DREAMMAKER

DEAN
EILERTSON

To Murray
FAIR WINDS
CALM SEAS

Dean

FriesenPress

Suite 300 - 990 Fort St
Victoria, BC, V8V 3K2
Canada

www.friesenpress.com

ISBN
978-1-5255-2793-7 (Hardcover)
978-1-5255-2794-4 (Paperback)
978-1-5255-2795-1 (eBook)

1. FICTION, COMING OF AGE

Distributed to the trade by The Ingram Book Company

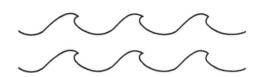

ROLL CREDITS.

FROM A BIRD'S EYE VIEW.

EXT. HIGHWAY – DAY

A Greyhound bus driving along Nova Scotia's narrow coastal highway heads south from Peggy's Cove towards Lunenburg.

SUPER: East Coast, Canada, 1948.

The bus continues on south through Mahone Bay, past two of the town's most beautiful churches, as the driver continues on his way up over a hill towards Chester. Chester's nine-hole golf course looks out over the first tee towards the Atlantic. Like a photo from a postcard, sailboats are out on the water taking advantage of the fresh spring breeze. By contrast, local fishermen work at their boats, laughing, waving to one another as them work away at unloading their freshly caught fish.

The squeaky sound of brakes being applied, as the bus comes to a stop. A young mother carrying bags of groceries continues onward as she crosses the road in front of the bus with her small son in tow.

Inside the bus, some passengers casually sit while others look out their windows checking out the people and sights. One of them, a handsome young man, looking slightly older than his age is 20-year-old DANIEL TANNER.

SUPER: Blue Rocks, Nova Scotia.

EXT. CEMETERY - DAY

A tiny, windswept county cemetery by the sea. A small funeral is in progress. One by one old gnarled hands pour soil over a pine casket as a minister recites from his bible. On Daniel, as he is gently coaxed forward with his own hand of soil.

EXT. BLUE ROCKS HARBOUR — LATE DUSK

An old pickup truck heads down a dusty road, towards a small two-storey house a quarter mile in the distance. The house has a slight lean to it, years of salt air and harsh Atlantic weather having taken their toll. From its knoll-top advantage, it overlooks the quiet sheltered bay of Blue Rocks.

The pickup stops; headlights light up the front porch. Daniel gets out on the passenger side; he's still dressed in the same clothes he was wearing at the funeral. Daniel struggles to lift his suitcase from the back of the truck. He does a 360 as he takes in his new surroundings. An older man, we'll soon know him as JOHN GREEK, turns off the ignition as he opens his rusty door. John reaches back in to grab his brown bag (full of beer) and a large legal-size envelope from inside the cab.

>   JOHN GREEK
> Well, I bet you haven't forgotten this
> ol' place.

Daniel continues to study the house as he nods. It's clear the place holds special memories for him.

INT. TANNER HOUSE - EVENING

The silence of the home's dusty rundown interior is broken as Daniel opens the front door, silhouetted in the entrance; he enters.

A second or two later, John enters shining his flashlight.

Daniel, suitcase in hand, appears to be familiar enough with his surroundings. He hoists his suitcase onto the sofa, finds a match dispenser, and lights a lantern.

John makes his way across the open room to the adjoining kitchen. He sets the bag of beer and the envelope on the kitchen table and then goes to the window over the kitchen sink and gives it a tug.

> JOHN GREEK
> All this place needs is a bit of fresh
> air and some cleaning. Geez, these
> windows must be painted shut
> or somethin'.

As John turns his attention back to the table, he reaches into the brown bag, pulls out a beer, uses the edge of the table to open it, and sets it on the table as he motions to Daniel that it's for him.

Daniel joins John in the kitchen as he grabs his beer. Together they survey the room as John opens a second beer and takes a swig.

> JOHN GREEK (CONT'D)
> I'd say ol' Jim really liked his mess.
> Here's to a sad day. Glad you were
> able to make it.

They clink bottles.

JOHN GREEK (CONT'D)

That's life I s'pose. Now it's all up
to you to carry on the fine Tanner
name. We gonna look at these papers
or not?

INT. KITCHEN — MOMENTS LATER

Daniel takes another swig from his beer then carefully sets it down
on the table. The overhead china hat light, with its downward glow,
isolates the two men from the rest of the room as together they
start looking over ol' Jim's legal papers.

JOHN GREEK (CONT'D)

This here is your granddad's will.
Says he is of sound mind. Says he
has "elected" to leave everything to
Daniel Tanner. Or last remaining.

DANIEL

That's me!? Everything!?

Daniel with a surprised, confused look once again takes in the
shabby look of his surroundings.

JOHN GREEK

Hold on there, boy. I think that
means this house, the land it sits
on, an' everything else. Including
that piece of scrap outside he called
a truck.

Daniel calculates his new reality as he takes a more realistic look
around at his inheritance.

DANIEL
You mean me and the mice. How
much do you think I could get for
this place?

JOHN GREEK
Two bits if you're lucky. Most folks is
leavin' if they can. Even the fish.

He laughs as he sneaks a quick look at his watch, all the while calmly downing what's left of his beer. He then reaches in to the bag for another.

INT. LIVING ROOM — MOMENTS LATER

Daniel clears a space, so he can sit. In the process, he accidentally knocks over a small side table. His grandfather's pipes, an old tobacco tin full of ash and burnt matches, photos in old wooden frames all go flying.

JOHN GREEK (CONT'D)
Easy there, son. Don't go breakin'
stuff you can't fix. Those probably be
the only prize possessions ol' Jim had.

Daniel stoops down to clean up the mess. He blows some ash off a faded picture collage featuring a photo of him as a boy. Next to it is a family picture taken in happier times, with young Daniel sitting on his grandfather's lap. Finally, a portrait of Daniel's father in his army uniform, proudly standing beside his grandmother out in front of the house. Broken glass falls from the frame to reveal a clearer view.

DANIEL

That's it, isn't it? This is all that's left.
These old pictures and me.

INT. TANNER HOUSE - MORNING

Daniel looks like he has barely slept. It's a nice day outside. He
throws open the front door to air out the place. The place doesn't
look half bad with the curtains pulled open; this could be okay!

INT. MOLLY'S RESTAURANT - MORNING

Daniel sits by himself smoking a cigarette as he sips his coffee.
Three old men are sitting at the counter chatting about things older
men chat about. BILL JOHANSEN sits at a table across from Daniel,
eating his hearty breakfast. Bill is a local retired fisherman. The
years of hard work and salty air have kept him fit yet weathered. He
still has a youthful twinkle in his eyes. Daniel recognizes him from
the funeral.

BILL JOHANSEN

Morning.

DANIEL

Mornin'! My name's --

BILL JOHANSEN

Daniel. I know. I used to bounce
you on my knee when you was just a
wee fry.

DANIEL

I'm sorry, I don't remember yours.

BILL JOHANSEN
Bill Johansen. I fished with
your granddad.

Daniel laughs nervously as he butts out his smoke.

DANIEL
That right?

BILL JOHANSEN
Jim was a good friend. One of the
last of the original sea captains from
these parts. We're going ta miss
ol' Jim. We all gotta go sometime,
I suppose.

An awkward beat.

BILL JOHANSEN (CONT'D)
So, what are yer plans?

DANIEL
Just staying long enough to sort a
few things out, clean up some of his
affairs. Then probably head back up
to Halifax.

BILL JOHANSEN
Sounds like a plan. Worse places a
fellow could hang his hat, I suppose.

DANIEL
I'm going to need some kind of work
to tide me over while I'm here. Any

chance a fella might get work on one
of those cannery boats?

> BILL JOHANSEN
>
> Just tell folks who you are. Being a
> Tanner in this town will always open
> doors for ya.

Both men fall silent as they sip their coffee. Bill starts to take one
of his homemade cigarettes out of a plastic case.

> DANIEL
>
> Here, have one of my tailor-mades.

> BILL JOHANSEN
>
> Thanks, no. Don't want ta get
> spoiled now.

Bill spits a piece of loose tobacco off his tongue, coughs a deep
rumbling cough, takes another drink of coffee, then flicks a match
to light up his cigarette.

> BILL JOHANSEN (CONT'D)
>
> I got a nephew works at the NSP
> yards. He's about your age. You could
> give him a call.

MOLLY, the waitress, in her 60s, arrives with Daniel's breakfast.

> MOLLY
>
> You want more coffee?

Daniel motions for more. Bill smiles a toothless grin as he pushes
his cup closer for the fifth refill.

                    BILL JOHANSEN
             Thanks, Molly. Just warm it up a bit.

                    DANIEL
             I vaguely remember him. That was a
             long time ago.

                    BILL JOHANSEN
             I know NSP has been hiring. If you
             want, like I said, he can put in a word
             for ya.

                    DANIEL
             I don't know how long any of this is
             going to take or whether I'm really
             staying or not.

Daniel starts in on his breakfast, savouring his first bite as he looks
out the window towards the harbour.

                    BILL JOHANSEN
             It's not like you've come from away, is
             it now? You're a Tanner. You belong
             right here. Get some of this good
             salt air in your lungs will do ya good.
             You'll see.

                    DANIEL
             I already got a job up in Halifax
             -- that is if I can get back there soon
             enough. I just need something to tide
             me over.

Bill takes another sip from his coffee.

BILL JOHANSEN

Maritimers have a saying here. "The
sea's in my veins, an' my blood is part
salt..." Being a Tanner, you'll see, boy.
You spend any time here, you won't
be headin' back up to Halifax. I'd even
put money on it.

Bill finishes his coffee, pushes his plate aside, pockets some sugar
packs, as he stands up.

BILL JOHANSEN (CONT'D)

I'll get my nephew to give you a
call then.

DANIEL

Thanks. Nice talkin' to ya.

BILL JOHANSEN

See ya around, son. Good luck.

Bill nods goodbye as he heads towards the till, counting out whatever he has left in his pocket to pay for breakfast.

As he heads towards the cashier, Bill stops to say hi to his old
friends still sitting at the counter. As they talk, a couple of them
look back towards Daniel. With a couple of nods, a few bucks
make their way to Bill as their conversation comes to an end.

BILL JOHANSEN

Thanks, boys, means a lot. Hey,
Molly, that Tanner kid's breakfast is
on us today.

He slaps his money down, pointing towards Daniel.

EXT. MOLLY'S RESTAURANT - MORNING

The morning fog is still quite thick.

Daniel heads across the street towards his grandfather's old pickup truck. Its original factory lines have been replaced by wood wherever the metal has lost the battle against the salt.

EXT. GROCERY STORE - DAY

The sun has finally started to burn through the fog. Daniel exits the store carrying a box of groceries. He places them in the box of his truck.

INT. DANIEL'S TRUCK - DAY

Daniel releases the handbrake. The pickup slowly starts to roll downhill. Hand on the stick shift in first gear, he expertly pops the clutch using gravity to start the truck. Black exhaust belches out as the engine backfires; the truck continues with a lurch as it heads down the hill towards the water. A typical Lunenburg morning, in the distance, cannery boats are heading out to sea.

EXT. TANNER HOUSE — LATE AFTERNOON

Daniel is out on the porch, trying to repair a broken window. He stops for a second and surveys an offshore fog bank.

> JIM SR. (V.O.)
> Daniel, you're fourth-generation
> Tanner. You can be proud of that.
> You're from one of the toughest

sea-goin' families of fishin' men dese
parts have ever known. If ya never
got nothing else, you'll always have
your name and your pride. Believe it
or not, this will always be your home.

FLASHBACK EXT. SIDE YARD - DAY

YOUNG DANIEL runs towards JIM SR. and his father, JIM JR., carrying
a pail full of fresh mussels.

> YOUNG DANIEL
> Grandma said we can cook these for
> dinner. They're "muscles." I found
> them under the boat shed where you
> told me!

> JIM SR.
> That's quite a feed you got us dere,
> Daniel. Now take 'em up to yer
> Moma. I bet she'll cook us up a real
> fine chowder with 'em.

> YOUNG DANIEL
> Grandpa, you says there's a whole
> world out there behind that fog. Can
> you take me there tomorrow?

> JIM SR.
> Well son, it ain't that easy it takes
> a long time to get to where that is.
> Tomorrow she might just decide ta
> throw our boat back onto her shores.

Lots of men have died or been lost
out there for less.

                    YOUNG DANIEL
Are you scared?

                    JIM SR.
Na, I'm not scared. Jus' let me tell ya.
Any man that thinks he can go out
on those there waters for no good
reason is jus' plain taunting her.

Having heard Jim Sr.'s explanation to Daniel, Jim Jr. playfully
messes Daniel's hair and looks back at his father, Jim Sr. This topic
has obviously been the source of tensions in the past.

                    JIM JR.
It takes a special man like your
grandpa to love the sea, accepting
her the way she is. Life's not up to us.
You'll learn you can't take what the
sea isn't willing to give.

Jim Jr. looks up at the sky.

                    JIM JR. (CONT'D)
Besides I'd rather be up there in the
sky. I've read we'll have aero planes
someday that will take us to where
ever we want to go.

                                        END FLASHBACK

Daniel gets up from the porch and heads down a slope towards a shed built out on the rocks by the water. A crudely built gangway, in total disrepair, leads to it. Scattered about are piles of old lobster traps, markers, and nets. A bent nail holds the shed door shut. With one twist, the door swings open.

INT. SHED - DAY

Frozen in time, the interior is a vivid display of Tanner Sr.'s life. Most obvious to the eye is his pale-yellow dory with forest-green trim, complete with freshly varnished oars. Rain gear and tools, worn by years of use, line the walls, each in its place. A calendar on the wall is dated October 1946.

EXT. SHED - DAY

The double doors let out a rusty squeak as they swing open, silhouetting Daniel in the opening; the dory sits patiently waiting behind him. Is Daniel really meant to be here?

Daniel disappears into the shed. The dory begins to move. Daniel pushes until the dory slides down its wooden ramp into the water; it's held by a weathered piece of cord. Daniel carefully steps aboard and checks for leaks and stability as he figures out how to fit the oars into the locks. He sits down for a second and then unties the knot and pushes off. He fumbles a bit but manages to get the dory moving forward.

EXT. BLUE ROCKS SHELTERED BAY — DAY

Daniel rows the dory parallel to shore.

EXT. SIDE YARD - DAY

Dean Eilertson

Daniel makes his way back up the path towards the house carrying a pail (the same pail as in the flashback) half full of mussels.

EXT. GRAVEL ROAD - DAY

Daniel gets out of his truck and reaches inside for his toolbox.

EXT. NATIONAL SEA PRODUCTS (NSP) REPAIR YARD - LATER

It's a busy place. Some 60 guys working away, with Daniel in the mix.

> YOUNG WORKMAN
> The real money to be made is out there, not here.

He motions towards the sea.

> JOSEF SORENSEN
> That's if you got a skipper who knows the waters. You don't get paid if you come home with a empty hold.

> DANIEL
> What? You saying if a guy works his tail off and don't catch fish, he don't get paid?

> JOSEF SORENSEN
> Yep! At least here you know you're takin' somethin' home every Friday. Hand me that sledge.

YOUNGER WORKMAN
Couple years ago, those boys was
makin' a fortune!

JOSEF SORENSEN
How soon ya forget. It was only
the worst year in maritime history.
Fifteen men from here dead. Shit,
your da was one of them, and your
Uncle Carl!

Daniel listens, looks out to sea. Still, it's all so alluring just the same.

Josef picks up a huge sledgehammer, looks to where Daniel is looking, then goes back to focusing on work, aiming powerful hits to a stubborn piece of cribbing.

EXT. BLUE ROCKS SHELTERED BAY - DAY

A Cape Breton jig plays as Daniel rows his dory towards a marker. He's dressed in his grandfather's old rain gear and looks to be quite seasoned compared to the last time we saw him. He gaffs a floating marker into the boat and pulls in on a line attached to a lobster trap. A couple of nice sized lobsters are inside.

He reaches inside only to get snapped at. He tries shaking the trap upside down. The little guys cling to the netting on the sides. Daniel closes the trap and sets it down. He takes up the oars as he starts rowing back towards shore with his dinner.

EXT. TANNER HOUSE - DAY

A second truck is parked outside the house.

Bill stands leaning against the shed, smoking his pipe. Daniel waves as he approaches shore.

> BILL JOHANSEN
> I was driving by and saw the dory.
> For a minute, I thought you was
> ol' Jim come back to haunt poor
> Blue Rocks.

Daniel smiles.

> DANIEL
> No. Just trying my hand at catching
> some dinner.

Daniel tosses his line. Bill catches it and starts to haul him in.

Daniel pulls in his oars, climbs out of his dory, and proudly hoists the trap.

> DANIEL (CONT'D)
> If I had known you were comin' by,
> I'd a caught a few more.

> BILL JOHANSEN
> Pay no mind. I was just being neigh-
> bourly. My nephew says your work
> at the yards is goin' pretty good. Nice
> gettin' a pay pack once in a while,
> I'm sure.

                    DANIEL
        No complaints. Those sure are a great
        bunch a guys. Thank you again for
        putting my name in.

EXT. TANNER BOAT SHED

They head towards the house. Daniel struggles to carry the lobster
trap under his arm. (They weigh 60 pounds.)

                    BILL JOHANSEN
        Are you goin' ta get yar dinner out of
        dar, or you plannin' to cook 'em in dat
        damn trap?

Reddening slightly, Daniel looks at the trap and shrugs.

                    DANIEL
        I thought I'd figure that out when I
        got up to the house.

Bill grins from ear to ear.

                    BILL JOHANSEN
        You means to say ya don't know
        how to get dose lobster out an' onto
        your plate!?

                    DANIEL
        No, no, I figured I'd get a pot with a
        lid and --

With one of his huge laughs, Bill grabs the trap out of Daniel's
arms, sets it down, and reaches into his pocket for his pocket knife.

He cuts four wedges off a twig and grips them in the corner of his mouth. He then opens the little door on the trap; he sticks the twig inside. When he lifts the twig back out, a lobster is clinging to it by one claw. With his free hand, he presses a wedge into the hinge part of each claw and then hands the twig and the lobster to Daniel. The whole process takes just a few seconds.

> BILL JOHANSEN
> Thar ya go! Just remember, don't eat
> those little bits of wood.

He pinches a piece of skin on either side of his neck and pulls to give the impression that something is stuck in his throat. Then he lets out another tremendous toothless laugh.

Daniel grins sheepishly.

> DANIEL
> There you go, rubbin' in my city
> upbringin'. Can I at least get you
> a beer? Come on, I got a couple in
> the icebox.

INT. TANNER HOUSE – DAY

Bill steps inside, as his eyes adjust, he gazes around. Only the space between the living room and the kitchen looks lived in. The rest of the place is still like the day Daniel arrived. He's obviously been sleeping on the sofa. His suitcase lies open on a nearby stool, a string of socks and underwear hang across one side of the room near the heater.

Daniel is embarrassed.

DANIEL

I got to admit, it's real strange living
in another man's place. Feels like I'm
only visiting or somethin'. Let me get
you that beer.

Daniel heads towards the ice box, setting the lobster in the sink on
his way.

BILL JOHANSEN

Okay, one for the road I suppose.

Bill heads towards a bookcase, accepting the beer while surveying
the assortment of books.

BILL JOHANSEN (CONT'D)

I hope you haven't brought a girl
back to this dump. If you did, you've
likely scared her off for good.

DANIEL

It hasn't sunk in yet that this place
is mine. It's going to take time,
you know.

BILL JOHANSEN

So, what's your point? Ya got to be
like the rest of us ol' dogs. Lift yar
leg. Make your mark! Stake yer turf.

Uneasily Daniel laughs.

    BILL JOHANSEN (CONT'D)
  Ol' Jim had his time here, and now
  it's up to you to breathe some new
  life into dese here walls. You know
  what I mean thar, boy?

Bill pulls a captain's log from a shelf and opens it.

    BILL JOHANSEN (CONT'D)
  No man can live in the shadow of
  another. That's life.

He replaces the ledger, sips his beer, looks at the other books on the shelves.

    BILL JOHANSEN (CONT'D)
  There's some interesting readin' here.
  I wouldn't be too quick on losing
  any of these if you're t'all interested
  in history.

EXT. TANNER HOUSE – EVENING

Daniel watches Bill back up and then stop.

    BILL JOHANSEN (CONT'D)
  Enjoy your lobster. See ya 'round.

They exchange waves. Bill drives off down the narrow, dusty road, his truck's headlights sending arcs of light out over the desolate landscape as he heads out towards the main road.

EXT. TANNER HOUSE – DAY

Daniel has taken Bill's advice. A radio plays LOUD MUSIC, accompanied by the sounds of cleaning, sweeping, and sneezing as clouds of dust spew out the open windows.

The screen door swings open, and Daniel appears carrying a box of junk. He throws it into the back of his truck. It's full of newspapers, rags, and broken, worn-out stuff, nothing of interest or value. He heads back in for more.

INT. TANNER HOUSE - NIGHT

Daniel emerges from the bathroom wearing a towel around his waist while he dries his hair with another. He heads upstairs.

INT. BEDROOM - NIGHT

Weary from cleaning, Daniel sits on the edge of the bed clipping his toenails.

The bedroom is sparse with dated furniture. His clothes hang neatly in the closet, his suitcase finally stored away. Daniel gets into bed, fluffs up his pillow, and settles under the clean sheets. He looks around, lies back, lets out a huge sigh, and smiles to himself.

FADE TO:

INT. UPSTAIRS BEDROOM - NIGHT

Daniel is fast asleep. The lantern by his bed flickers as it runs out of fuel. The book he was reading before he fell asleep lies open beside him.

INSERT: HANDWRITTEN MESSAGE ON THE INSIDE COVER

To Jim Jr,
I spent my whole life on tall ships
chasing my dreams. . .
may the day come when you with
your dreams find the sea.
Merry Christmas,
Christmas 1929

The title of the book is *Moby Dick*.

EXT. NSP REPAIR YARD — EARLY MORNING

SUPER: Five months later.

Tradesmen arrive for work. Daniel pulls up in his truck. He has lost his baby fat and replaced it with muscle. He makes his way towards the time shack. A big, bright poster is tacked on the notice board alongside the usual for-sale ads and bulletins. Daniel stops to take it in. It says, "Annual Lunenburg summer fair! Games, cooking contests, bake sale, dory races, mast climbing and prizes."

Workers continue past, punching their time cards as they go. Few take notice of Daniel staring at the dory race pictured on the poster, except for Josef.

> JOSEF SORENSEN
> Ya think you can carry on the
> Tanner tradition?

> DANIEL
> What's that?

JOSEF SORENSEN
That's your da out in front there. I
think he was still champ when he
shipped out overseas.

Daniel looks at Josef and then turns back to the poster.

EXT. NSP REPAIR YARD – MORNING

Midway through the morning break, Josef is caught up in telling a
few of the others one of his old, salty stories for the twentieth time.

JOSEF SORENSEN
. . . gigging for fish in that godfor-
saken freezing cold. I'm covered in
ice, freezing my arse. Try rowing
a dory full a cod back to your
ship when she's flat calm. Damn
near impossible! Now I'm out in
this fuckin' squall rowin', so damn
scared, ya know? So fuckin' afraid I
was going to lose sight of da main
ship. Christ, if I don't get my dory
swamped! This buddy of mine
forgettin' his own life, ya know?
Gets turned back around, an' here he
comes rowin' back to me! No medals
for bravery in those days, just the
thanks in my eyes. Come ta think
there, it was Daniel's da saved me
that day. Brave man -- poor bastard.
Like they say, that was the way
back then. He knew I'd have done
the same for him. You know what I

mean? Then we'd head her back out
the next morning to do the same
damn thing all over again. Christ!
Makes a man wonder.

All the while, Daniel has been within earshot of the whole conversation. As Josef walks towards him:

DANIEL

I didn't know you knew my dad.

JOSEF SORENSEN

Oh, for sure, boy. Your da was as
good a Tanner as they come.

DANIEL

I hardly knew the man myself.
I never got a chance to even say
goodbye when my mum took with
me and headed up to Dartmouth.

JOSEF SORENSEN

Ya an' that day just about killed him.
I'm tellin' ya, Jim was a good man.
He gave his life for God and country
never askin' for anything in return.

DANIEL

Once mum took off for Toronto,
I was pretty much left to fend for
myself. I stopped expectin' much.

                    JOSEF SORENSEN
          Jim was so damn proud to have a son
          like you, schoolin' to be someone he
          thought he never was. Always was
          bragging 'bout you.

Daniel's shoulders slump down. Josef towers over him.

                 JOSEF SORENSEN (CONT'D)
          I know the poor bugger was so scared
          that you was ashamed to have him as
          a pa. Sometimes I think that's why he
          went off an' joined.

Josef throws what's left of his coffee into the water.

Daniel is dumbstruck. Josef is hard-pressed to control his feelings.

                        DANIEL
          I did too! We just never spoke.

                    JOSEF SORENSEN
          Kiss my arse, an' shut your mout! I
          was having a good day here till you
          brought this up. Breaks over. Back
          ta work!

EXT. NSP REPAIR YARD - DAY

Work is finished on an old trawler in for repairs. Men are busy
getting ready to break away the blocks and let her slip back into the
water. It's a huge task with lots of yelling by Josef, who oversees the
operation. The rusty hull towers over the men. They pound wedges
with their sledgehammers to slowly lift the ugly old beast off its

blocks. Finally, it starts to slide down the ramp towards the water. Under its massive weight, spray flies up over the ship's bow, obscuring it.

Daniel collects an arm load of wedges; out on the water the trawler makes its way into the harbour. Josef's gnarled, dirty hand lands on Daniel's shoulder.

> JOSEF SORENSEN
> Great work, boys! Let's call it a day!
> Daniel, I'll be havin' a word with ya
> before you leave.

Daniel straightens up, covered in filth. Sweat drips from his brow, his singlet dirty and soaked with sweat.

> DANIEL
> This 'bout my work?

> JOSEF SORENSEN
> No, your work's fine. I just wanted to
> talk a bit more 'bout yesterday.

Josef pats another guy on the shoulder as he walks by.

> JOSEF SORENSEN (CONT'D)
> Thanks, Sam. Good work.

Josef turns, picks up his tools, and heads up towards the massive NSP repair building (where they built the original Bluenose).

Daniel, finishes stacking wedges, then follows after him.

EXT. PARKING LOT - DAY

Daniel leans against his pickup having a smoke. Josef approaches. He's in a friendlier mood.

> JOSEF SORENSEN
> Don't matter how many boats I
> send down those ramps, it's always a
> great sight.

(points at the trawler)

> Nice to be done with that piece of
> scrap. Somethin' wrong 'bout a boat
> from Newfoundland tryin' to work
> these waters. Jus' stupid.

> DANIEL
> She's built fine.

> JOSEF SORENSEN
> She's built for a different place. The
> seas don't run the same down here.
> If you come from away, things is
> always different.

> DANIEL
> What are you leading to? You think I
> don't belong here either?

> JOSEF SORENSEN
> Actually, I was going to say how
> havin' a Tanner back here in the yards
> brings back some good memories.
> Your granddad skippered the first
> schooner for NSP. Your old man

worked here for years. A lot of good
men did, including my son.

> DANIEL
>
> One of the boys was sayin' - your son
> went off overseas to fight.

> JOSEF SORENSEN
>
> Yeah, my son fought -- an' died. He
> was killed in Belgium in forty-one.
> Seven years ago today. My son was
> everything to me. Your dad lost you
> in a different way. He used to brag so
> much about you.

> DANIEL
>
> At least you knew your son. Wish I
> could say the same for my dad.

Josef shakes his head.

> JOSEF SORENSEN
>
> Son, I'm tryin' ta tell ya nicely. Your
> father went off to that fuckin' war,
> all the time hopin' he'd make it
> back to find a son who was proud
> of him. Poor bastard figured you
> was too ashamed to have him for
> a father. Being a Maritimer wasn't
> good enough.

Daniel's eyes start to well up.

DANIEL

I was proud of him! I just wish I
knew him is all.

JOSEF SORENSEN

Look, we lost a whole generation to
that war, my son included, an' dere's
no more after me. You've come back.
It's all Jim ever wanted, got it?

The two go to shake hands. Josef pulls Daniel in and gives him a
strong one-armed hug. Daniel watches as Josef walks away.

JOSEF SORENSEN (CONT'D)

You sleep on that. We'll see
you tomorrow.

EXT. GRAVEYARD - DUSK

Daniel stands in front of his grandfather's grave. The soil covering
it has already settled. To one side of his grandfather's and grandmother's headstones is a bronze plaque with a picture of Jim Jr. in
uniform. Beneath are inscribed the dates "1917-1944" along with
a quote '

"One man's dreams are another man's reality." -- Jules Verne.

DANIEL (V.O.)

The more I learned about my family,
the more I respected them for
their strength.

Daniel drops to his knees, he starts pulling out some of the weeds
growing around the graves. Remorsefully, he shakes his head.

Dean Eilertson

DANIEL (V.O.) (CONT'D)
Folks from around here have so much
pride, yet to them, that's never good
enough. So much so, most even feel
shame for who they are.

INT. TANNER HOUSE, ATTIC - NIGHT

Daniel sets down a few empty boxes and then grabs the handles of
an old trunk up on a shelf and hoists it down to the floor. He wipes
off some of the dust then opens the lid. The contents are like gold.
He can't believe what he just found.

DISSOLVE TO:

SAME SCENE — EARLY DAWN

Daniel has been up all night. Assorted bits lie neatly spread out
in front of him. Scrapbooks full of photos, his father's old report
cards, ribbons won for rowing, a mariner's knife, assorted letters
and papers, a set of keys, a well-worn sou'wester (hard as nails), a
navigator's sexton, and a captain's cap. Daniel sits looking at a small
open box holding his father's service medals.

DANIEL (V.O.)
That night I found an old deed
describing "one building with land,
Lot 129, in the Municipality of
Chester." It was made out to James
Earl Tanner, free of all liens and
encumbrances, dated August 5, 1930.
It had been notarized in Chester by
Circuit Judge Collins. Price paid back
then was one hundred dollars.

EXT. NSP REPAIR YARD - DAY

Daniel is young; the work is hard. He's tired from the night before and looks it. The lunch whistle blows. Daniel motors out of the parking lot.

INT. CHESTER TOWN HALL - DAY

Daniel approaches the reception desk.

> RECEPTIONIST
> Yes, young man, how can I help you?

> DANIEL
> Yes. How do I find out whether this
> piece of paper is still worth somethin'
> or not?

> RECEPTIONIST
> May I?

She takes the document and examines it under her glasses.

> RECEPTIONIST (CONT'D)
> This appears to be legitimate. The seal
> here is ours. This here judge passed
> away some time ago. All I can check
> for you today is who pays the taxes. If
> you have a few minutes, it shouldn't
> take long.

She heads to the back. Daniel is left standing there. A few people come and go. Moments later, the receptionist returns holding a file, a note stapled to the front.

RECEPTIONIST (CONT'D)
It says here the taxes are overdue.
There's also this returned letter
marked "deceased."

DANIEL
That right? I've been marking everything addressed to him "deceased."
Thought that was what you're supposed to do.

RECEPTIONIST
In these cases, we are forced by law to
hold such deeds for ten years or until
next-of-kin are notified. Are you
related to the deceased?

DANIEL
Yes. That's my granddad. I got this
will that says he left me all his things.

Daniel hands it to her.

RECEPTIONIST
In these cases, you are required by
law to fill out a transfer-of-ownership
form with proof of your identification
notarized by a lawyer.

DANIEL
How much is this property worth?

RECEPTIONIST

I'm sorry son, the law does not allow
me to give out that information.

DANIEL

How much is owing in taxes?

RECEPTIONIST

I'm sorry, but the law --

DANIEL

-- Doesn't permit you to give out that
kind of information. This is some real
fine needle threadin', isn't it? I don't
know how much the land is worth,
and I don't know the taxes owed,
but the law wants me to do all these
things before it will permit me to
know anything else about a property
that's supposed to be mine in the
first place.

RECEPTIONIST

There are very strict rules to
protect owners' rights. Do you own
other properties?

DANIEL

Just the house and land he already
left me.

RECEPTIONIST

So, you already know the procedure then.

Daniel frowns in confusion.

> DANIEL
> You mean I got to do that with what
> I got already?

> RECEPTIONIST
> Yes, of course. We have to keep
> records. How else do we know who
> to send the tax bill to?

> DANIEL
> Taxes? I got to pay taxes?

> RECEPTIONIST
> Not until it's officially yours. For now,
> the county only knows that there
> is a deceased title holder. Without
> the proper paperwork, ownership
> will eventually be passed over to the
> Crown. I get the impression that you
> haven't done any of this. I suggest you
> have your father contact a --

> DANIEL
> I don't have a father. He was killed
> -- in the war.

Daniel struggles to control his emotions.

> RECEPTIONIST
> Then all I can suggest is you take
> these forms and find a lawyer who
> can help you.

                    DANIEL
          How long does all this take? And
          how much will it cost?

                  RECEPTIONIST
          Usually four to six weeks. The
          expenses incurred will be between
          you and your lawyer.

Daniel turns to leave. Other people wait patiently in line
behind him.

              RECEPTIONIST (CONT'D)
          Sir! You forgot your transfer forms!
          Next in line, please.

Daniel turns back, takes the forms along with his grandfather's will
and leaves.

INT. LAWYER'S OFFICE - DAY

Daniel is signing documents.

                    LAWYER
          These are the transfers of title for
          your grandfather's land titles. This
          document transfers his other assets,
          his bank account, government bonds,
          federal fishing licences, and finally,
          this is for the motor vehicle branch,
          so you can license his truck.

                            DANIEL

Life was pretty easy till you came
along. I've never seen so much paper.

                            LAWYER

Laws, rules, and paperwork have
always existed, son. It's just taken
you a while to discover them. You
should be thankful your grandfather
even had a will. If the feds had gotten
involved, the added costs would have
forced you to walk away from the
whole lot. As it is, he left just enough
funds in place to cover all of these
bills. Almost forgot, here's mine.

Of course, the lawyer's last stab is his bill. Daniel looks at the bill in
one hand and a sheet totalling his assets in the other.

                            DANIEL

You're barely leaving me with the
shirt on my back!

The lawyer smiles as if Daniel's comment were a compliment.

                            LAWYER

Mr. Tanner, transferring land titles
and closing out wills are not easy
matters. Trust me. The good side is
now you get to pay taxes like the rest
of us. Welcome to the real world.

He holds out his hand to shake Daniel's. Daniel eyes him back
in frustration.

EXT. ROAD - DAY

Daniel drives his pickup down a road known as 2nd peninsula. Along the way are assorted homes and sheds.

INT. DANIEL'S TRUCK - DAY

Daniel looks out at landmarks as he follows his hand drawn map as he drives.

EXT. ROAD - DAY

Daniel passes a dirt driveway. He stops. Backs up. Looks at his map. Decides to pull in.

INT. TRUCK - DAY

To one side stands a large shed with a small quite inlet beyond. Daniel gets out of his truck and makes his way down a path over grown with brambles.

EXT. SHED - DAY

Vines of brambles grow up the front of the building. He can just make out a door. It's locked with a brass padlock.

Daniel pulls out the set of keys he found in the trunk up in the attic. It has been a long time since this lock was last opened. Daniel gives the key a hard turn. It opens with a dry, raspy click. Daniel takes the lock from its hasp as he starts to push open the door.

INT. SHED - DAY

Beams of light shine through cracks in the wall boards, revealing various dark shapes.

Daniel walks the length of the shed. A narrow path down one side leads towards an open area at the far end framed with a pair of big double doors. He fumbles with the latch. The weight of the doors swing them outwards. In the blinding light, a ramp similar to the kind used to launch boats at the repair yard slopes down towards the water. Daniel turns around. He sees an unpainted rudder still clamped in C-clamps, rough scarfs of live oak lay neatly stacked against one wall. Off to the side is a workbench. On the wall over the bench are neatly hung shipbuilding tools.

He approaches the workbench and unrolls a set of hand-drawn plans; every drawing reveals more detail. Pencilled calculations and reminder notes are tacked up on the wall behind the bench. This well-organized work space echoes his grandfather's own shed back at Blue Rocks. Only everything in this shed has to do with boats, woodwork, or carpentry. A ledger-sized book rests on a shelf over the workbench. A handwritten title is scribed on its cover.

> DANIEL (V.O.)
> Dreammaker.

Daniel opens the ledger. On the inside page is the same quote as on his father's headstone.

> DANIEL (V.O.) (CONT'D)
> "One man's dreams are another
> man's reality."

Daniel turns the page.

DANIEL (V.O.) (CONT'D)
"Our dream is to sail around the
world. Together we will make this
dream our reality. The boat we build
will be called Dreammaker. May
God give us strength. James Daniel
Tanner, October 21st, 1932."

Canvas tarpaulins hang off a 50-foot-long form that fills the length
of the shed. The first dusty tarp hits the floor, revealing a smoothly
planed, finely crafted stern.

Daniel touches the beautiful wood, every joint is precisely fitted,
wooden dowels pinning each plank. The overall impression is that
whoever was working here just might return and pick up where
they left off.

Daniel continues pulling off the tarps as he reveals the rear cockpit.
The layout is modern by design; all leads for the blocks lead back
into the cockpit. Daniel stands back as he surveys the layout.

EXT. ROAD - DAY

Daniel is driving, grinning like a little kid. On the seat beside him
is the ledger.

EXT. BLUE ROCKS SHELTERED BAY - DAY

The bow of Daniel's pale-yellow dory slices through the water. Oars
cut forcefully down into the icy black sea as Daniel pulls hard. A
lobster boat approaches the entrance into the protected bay's calmer
waters. Daniel waves. The boat changes direction towards him.

Dean Eilertson

John is at the controls. He backs off on the throttle and brings his boat to a stop. Daniel's dory nudges up against it. Daniel grabs the side.

> DANIEL
> You'll never guess what I just found!

John frowns with confusion.

> JOHN GREEK
> What ya lose?

The motion of the sea rising and falling, both men strain to hang on to each other's craft.

> DANIEL
> A boat! My dad's boat!

> JOHN GREEK
> Right. A boat. Son, forgive me. I
> may be losing a bit of me mind, but
> I haven't got a cod jigger's clue what
> yar talkin' 'bout.

> DANIEL
> It's one they were building. I think
> it's a sailboat!

One swell too many, and the two lose their grip. The next moment, they are adrift, 10 to 15 feet apart.

> DANIEL (CONT'D)
> Come by later!

Half losing his balance, Daniel settles back onto the bench and takes up his oars.

> JOHN GREEK
> It's gettin' rough out here. Do ya want
> a tow back in? What ya doin' out
> here anyways?

> DANIEL
> Training for the fair!

John signals he can't hear.

> DANIEL (CONT'D)
> For the fair!

Doing his best Marcel Marceau, Daniel exaggerates his rowing.

No luck either way in understanding each other, the two go about their business. John hits the throttle as the trawler belches out black exhaust. Daniel, with powerful well-coordinated strokes, heads off, a different figure than when he first tried his hand at rowing.

The bow of Daniel's dory slices through the water as he pulls the oars with powerful rhythmic strokes.

The distant roar of CHEERING leads to. . .

EXT. LUNENBURG HARBOUR – DAY

Muscles glistening with sweat, Daniel looks back over his shoulder at other rowers hot in pursuit. It's fair day, just as described on the poster at the NSP repair yard. It's a dory race with Daniel in the lead. He crosses the finish line, exhausted.

The dory slices through the water. Ripples settle into reflections.

EXT. LUNENBURG HARBOUR - DAY

Daniel, covered in sweat, toasting with his race mates. A starter's cannon fires. The sound causes Daniel to jump.

> JOSEF SORENSEN
> Damn yacht race I don't know why
> they figure they can crash in on our
> fair. You?

> DANIEL
> Look as those boats. They're amazing!

Daniel watches with a new curiosity as sails are sheeted in. Crews pull on ropes while others shout out orders. Sweat continues to pour off Daniel's face. John yells down from the broad walk above.

> JOHN GREEK
> Way to go, champ! You just made me
> twenty bucks.

A beautiful, somewhat tarty local girl, GLORIA, laughs as she points out at a young man on one of the yachts. He's is having problems managing his jib line. Meet JAMES -- handsome, blond Harvard Law grad and captain of their famous rowing team. He is the kind of GQ man one might assume any woman would kill to be with. The skipper on board, RICHARD STEWART, is in his early 50s, Boston bred, strong, tanned, and a descendant of old money. Daniel watches as their jib flogs wildly in the wind, making incredibly loud flapping noises. Richard is forced to veer off leeward of his opponent. He is already losing ground and they've barely started to race.

RICHARD

Jesus H. Christ, grab hold of that
goddamn sheet and set the goddamn
jib, James! We're in the middle of a
race here!

Daniel heads up to join the others. He is immediately hit with the
spray from a beer one of his friends has shaken up and opened.

DANIEL

In my mouth! Don't waste it!

Tons of laughter as the locals celebrate. Gloria appears. She wraps
her arms around Daniel and gives him a kiss to end all kisses.

GLORIA

Congratulations, Daniel!

James takes in the cruel antics. Whoever she is kissing is stealing a
hug and grabbing her ass. She playfully responds by grinding her
hips into him. The other well-wishers pour beer over Daniel and
Gloria. She stares back coldly at James. She knows she's got his
jealous attention.

DANIEL

Still screwing with those rich boys
are ya, Gloria? Give it up. I know you
want me more.

GLORIA

Let go of me before I sack you one!
Is there no class among the lot of ya?

Daniel twirls her out of his arms and into the arms of someone who again spins her to someone else until she is spun right out of the group. They roar with laughter.

GLORIA (CONT'D)
Let go of me! Ya bunch of turds!

Older folks look on, frowning and shaking their heads with disapproval. Gloria stares them down with what little dignity she has left.

EXT. NSP REPAIR YARD - MORNING

Tattered ribbons left over from the weekend fair flutter in the breeze. Someone punches a time card. Richard's yacht is tied up to the repair yard dock, an ugly mess of busted planks and scarped paint along its starboard hull.

EXT. NSP REPAIR YARD - DAY

Richard's yacht is out of the water and up on blocks. Daniel is having his lunch on her deck. While he eats, he fusses around, touching the rigging, chrome winches, and so on.

With sandwich in mouth and hands on the wheel his moment of daydreaming is interrupted by the sound of someone clearing his throat. Like a dog caught helping itself to the family picnic, Daniel's look turns to embarrassment.

RICHARD
You always make a practice of playing
captain on other people's boats?

Daniel takes the sandwich out of his mouth.

                         DANIEL
          No, it's not what you think, sir. Not
          at all. Just never seen a sailboat like
          this before.

                        RICHARD
          Who's in charge of her repair?

                         DANIEL
          That'd probably be Smitty.

Richard takes in the information but is more interested in the
damage itself. He kneels down to get a better look.

                     DANIEL (CONT'D)
          If anyone can fix her, we can. Anyway,
          I'll go get the foreman for ya.

EXT. NSP REPAIR YARD - DAY

Richard talks with Josef and Smitty as Daniel and some of the
other men work at hauling a scallop boat out of the water.

                    YOUNG LABOURER
          These folks got more friggin' money
          than brains. All summer long, all they
          do is play on their damn boats and
          hang out at that stinkin' yacht club
          of theirs.

                         DANIEL
          Who is he?

YOUNG LABOURER

How the crap you 'spect me ta know?
Him and all the other rich buggers.

EXT. TANNER BOAT SHED – EVENING

Daniel's and John's trucks are parked out front. The lights are
on inside.

INT. TANNER BOAT SHED – EVENING

The two men are sitting in the boat's cockpit.

JOHN GREEK

No shortcuts, that's for sure. This
here is your granddad's mark. Every
peg wedged with African iron wood.
Christ, she's never going to shift in
any kind of weather.

DANIEL

I wonder what she's worth as
she stands?

JOHN GREEK

Don't even think about it! The sweat
alone that's gone into some of this
work is painful enough to think
about. Oh no, you got ta finish her.

DANIEL

Right! I haven't got the time or the
money, let alone the know-how to

even know where to start. Hell, I
don't even know how to sail!

JOHN GREEK
Then ya got some work to do,
don't ya, boy? The days when these
boats worked the seas, men from
these parts got pretty good at han-
dling them.

DANIEL
That's right, you've done some sailing!

JOHN GREEK
Let's just say them's the years I
remember the most.

John is caught up in silent thought for a moment, staring out at the
moonlit bay as he lights up his pipe.

JOHN GREEK (CONT'D)
You got yourself a damn fine
opportunity here, son. I wouldn't go
throwing it away just yet.

DANIEL
How much work do you honestly
think is left here, I mean, realistically?

JOHN GREEK
Lookin' at her, I'd say she's well
underway. Without bustin' yourself,
maybe a couple years.

                              DANIEL
              Then what, learn to sail it myself or
              sell it?

                           JOHN GREEK
              The only sailin' around here anymore
              is just down the road at that fancy
              yacht club. A smart fella like you
              gotta be able to least do as good
              as them.

John looks Daniel up and down and then laughs.

                     JOHN GREEK (CONT'D)
              Sorry. Just the picture of you standin'
              like you is down there among all
              those mucky-mucks.

                              DANIEL
              I don't know what you're gettin' at. I
              could sail if I wanted to. If I set my
              mind to it.

EXT. SHINY NEW CAR — EARLY MORNING

It's parked in an off-road clearing. Massachusetts licence plates.
Windows steamed up.

INT. SHINY NEW CAR — EARLY MORNING

In the back seat, James, his ass bare, is on top of Gloria, who is
half-naked, making out with total abandonment.

EXT. TANNER BOAT SHED — EARLY MORNING

The shed doors are open. For the first time, DREAMMAKER is completely uncovered. The shed is all neat and tidy. A pile of canvas tarpaulins in the foreground stirs. It's Daniel waking up.

EXT. OCEAN - MORNING

Yachts head across the bay. Richard's boat rounds one of the race course markers. At the helm, Richard smiles. His repaired yacht is in the lead! The next-closest yacht is well back. A young woman appears on deck and hands Richard a hot mug of coffee. It's Stewart's pride and joy, his only daughter, CANDACE. She's around the same age as Daniel.

> RICHARD
> Too bad James had to miss this race.
> I'm sure you'll be glad when those
> darn bar exams are over.

INT. TANNER BOAT SHED - MORNING

Daniel warms himself, taking in the radiant heat coming off his wood stove. He waits for the coffee percolator to do its thing.

EXT. TANNER BOAT SHED - MORNING

Daniel sits against a boulder, sipping his coffee and studying the race through his binoculars as he basks in the warm morning sun.

EXT. JAMES' CAR - MORNING

Back in the front seat, James and Gloria drive away.

EXT. OCEAN - MORNING

　　　　　Dean Eilertson

Candace's eyes take in the sleepy coastline with its salt shacks and fishing coves. Lazy smoke rises up from a few of the chimneys.

EXT. TANNER BOAT SHED - MORNING

Daniel sits up as he watches the race. He recognizes Richard's yacht out in front.

EXT. RICHARD'S YACHT - MORNING

Candace gazes pensively at the shoreline.

EXT. TANNER BOAT SHED - MORNING

Daniel standing in front of his shed staring back.

EXT. GLORIA'S HOUSE - MORNING

Gloria walks down her driveway as she fixes her tousled hair. A hedge up by the road obscures James' car as he drives away.

EXT. CHESTER YACHT CLUB — LATE AFTERNOON

From his truck on the side of the road, Daniel watches the yachts coming back in from the race. Sails are dropped. Ropes are tossed to crew who tie them to cleats on the docks. Others work at washing down the decks.

James pulls into the parking lot and makes a beeline down to the docks, smiling and waving.

                    JAMES
          How was your day?

> CANDACE

We won! You missed a great race.

> JAMES

That's great! Let's go celebrate.

> CANDACE

I can't just yet. We still have to fold
the sails and wash down the deck.

> JAMES

Candace, this is our last day together.
They surely won't mind this once.

Richard overhears their conversation and waves them off with
a nod.

> RICHARD

Go on, get out of here! Have a safe
trip back, James. We'll see you in a
few weeks. Good luck on your exams.

Candace grabs his hand, revealing her engagement ring.

> CANDACE

Come on. Let's go before he changes
his mind.

EXT. CHESTER YACHT CLUB PARKING LOT - DAY

James leans out of his car and honks to get Daniel's attention.
Candace turns red with embarrassment.

Dean Eilertson

                    JAMES
        Would you mind getting that wreck
        out of our parking lot!

Daniel, leaning against his truck and minding his own business, is
taken by surprise.

                    DANIEL
        Oh, sure. Sorry.

Daniel gets into his truck. Tries to start it. It turns over but won't
fire up.

James honks his horn impatiently.

                    JAMES
        Come on, you stupid moron, get off
        our property!

Finally, James pulls out and speeds past Daniel's truck.

James flips Daniel the finger as he drives off, leaving him in a cloud
of dust.

                    DANIEL
        What's your fuckin' problem?

EXT. CHESTER YACHT CLUB PARKING LOT - DAY

Dirty and oily, Daniel slams the hood of his truck. With a turn
of the key, oily black exhaust fills the air. Another car approaches.
Daniel tries desperately to get his truck into gear, fearing
another confrontation.

                    RICHARD
          Hey, aren't you from the repair yard?

                    DANIEL
          Yes, sir.

                    RICHARD
          Tell Smitty he did a hell of a job on
          my boat. It was going through gears
          today that I didn't know she had!

                    DANIEL
          I saw you out there in the lead earlier.
          She was sure movin'.

                    RICHARD
          Every time I sheeted her in, she'd
          squirt out that much faster. Be sure to
          tell him I can't thank him enough.

Daniel nods as he turns his attention back to backing up. Richard
honks his horn.

                    RICHARD (CONT'D)
          Wait! There's still a thing or two I'd
          like to get someone to look at. Would
          you know of anyone who might
          be interested?

                    DANIEL
          Yeah, I might.

                    RICHARD
          I'll pay for their time. You got a
          pencil? They can call whenever.
          Number is 5592. Name is Richard.

Daniel scribbles the number on a scrap of paper.

                    DANIEL
          Sounds good. Got it. I'll get him
          ta call ya. The man's name is John.
          John Greek.

                    RICHARD
          Thanks. I never caught your name.

Another car exiting the yacht club waits for Richard to pull out.

                    DANIEL
     Daniel.

Richard toots his horn and waves as he pulls away.

                    RICHARD
          Nice talking to you.

INT. TANNER BOAT SHED - DAY

John has stopped by with a few of his old boat-building tools
for Daniel.

                    JOHN GREEK
          That's just hunky dory! I like to know
          what gave you that notion.

John gives Daniel an annoyed look.

> DANIEL
> So, when are you goin' ta call him?

> JOHN GREEK
> I'm not callin' nobody.

> DANIEL
> Come on, John, he's even offering to
> pay ya!

> JOHN GREEK
> Sailing? With the likes of them?

> DANIEL
> I'll call him for ya then.

With Richard's number in hand, Daniel tries to hide the fact that he's begging John to phone. John knows it's Daniel's chance to get out on a sailboat. John smiles.

> JOHN GREEK
> You're always schemin', aren't ya, boy?
> You don't even got a phone.

John snatches the paper from Daniel's hand and puts it in his shirt pocket.

> JOHN GREEK (CONT'D)
> You're going to owe me for this one.

EXT. RICHARD'S YACHT - EVENING

It's a beautiful night. Cloud formations move across the sky. Richard is at the helm. John is talking, pointing, as the other two listen.

> JOHN GREEK
> Daniel you keep hanging on to that
> windward line. Now grab that jib
> sheet on your leeward side. Get her
> on dat der winch, set it hard, and get
> ready to ease out!

> RICHARD
> Tacking!

CUT TO:

An impressive tack. John shouts directions to Daniel.

> JOHN GREEK
> Now Daniel! Ease out! Good, now
> tie off!

> RICHARD
> You've got to show me that one
> again. She turned on a dime. That
> was amazing!

> JOHN GREEK
> You just got to remember to keep
> your main powered up right though
> the full turn. It's all in the timing.

> RICHARD
> You don't sail like that on fishing
> boats. Where did you learn that?

                    JOHN GREEK
          Let's just say there was a time when
          a few of us boys from around here
          used to give you Yanks a run for
          your money.

He winks. Daniel doesn't hear any of the conversation. He's up
near the bow coiling lines.

                      RICHARD
          What about Daniel? Are you train-
          ing him?

                    JOHN GREEK
          Nah, I'm too old for any that fool-
          ishness. He's got promise though,
          don't he?

                      RICHARD
          He sure seems to be enjoying himself.

EXT. CHESTER YACHT CLUB - NIGHT

The sun has set. Three figures stand on the dock. The sound of
slack lines and rigging chiming away as the wind blows through
the marina.

                      RICHARD
          Thank you both for coming out. John,
          you sure I can't talk you into coming
          out of retirement? We could use
          more local competition.

JOHN GREEK

No, Rick, I think I'll leave that to you young fellers.

Daniel gives John a look then mouths, "Rick?"

JOHN GREEK

Just keep workin' on those tacks like I told ya. Your zigzag problem, now that's most likely in your rudder mounts. Get them tightened up. That's distance lost, if you know what I mean. Otherwise, things checked out pretty good. Ya got a nice boat der.

RICHARD

Daniel, you seemed to handle things out there pretty well. If you're serious about learning more, just show up for our races. There's never enough crew. I'll make sure you get out with somebody.

DANIEL

Every Saturday and Sunday, right?

Richard's smile broadens.

RICHARD

That's right. Six a.m. sharp!

Daniel smiles. As does John. The lines have been crossed. Richard Stewart is an alright guy.

DANIEL

Thanks again, Mr. -- Richard, sir. I'll
be here!

INT. LEGION TAVERN - NIGHT

Smoky, loud local pub. Nothing fancy. Varnished plywood walls,
cheap beer, and pickled eggs.

JOHN GREEK

Cheers!

Draft glasses meet for a toast.

DANIEL

Ta yacht racin'!

Laughing, drinking. Daniel is so pumped!

DANIEL (CONT'D)

God, John, if you hadn't called him,
we -- I -- Did you see me on that
last tack? I didn't know what rope
was what!

JOHN GREEK

You just start draggin' yar sorry ass
out there on weekends like he said.
Rick's a good man. He knows his
sailing. He'll set you right.

INT. TANNER BOAT SHED - NIGHT

The wood stove crackling, Daniel works at mending a pair of fingerless wool gloves then turns to rubbing water-repellent wax into his sou'wester.

EXT. CHESTER YACHT CLUB - MORNING

Daniel sits on the grass with his canvas bag beside him, patiently waiting. People arrive, walk by with curious stares, awkward smiles and nods.

Richard pulls in, grabs his stuff and heads down towards the dock. A few of his crew are already at the boat. It looks like Daniel has been ignored.

> RICHARD
> Has anyone seen Daniel yet? He's
> that local kid I told you about.

One of them points up towards Daniel sitting on the grass. Richard cups his hands together over his mouth.

> RICHARD (CONT'D)
> Hey, Daniel! Come on, we're running
> late. Get the lead out!

Half the marina turns to see who he's yelling at.

Daniel gets up and heads towards the boat. DEAN takes each of the crew members' bags and stows them below.

> DEAN
> Chad! Candace! Check this guy out.

Even though their ages are close, their hairstyles and clothes obviously are not.

> RICHARD
>
> Guys, I'd like you to meet Daniel.
> He's going to be sailing with us when
> he can. Daniel, this here is my son,
> Dean. That's Chad, and poking her
> head up out from the galley is my
> daughter, Candace.

Dean's soft hands meet Daniel's strong hands in a handshake. CHAD's face is round compared to Daniel's more defined features. Candace looks mature compared to Daniel's innocence. She looks into his eyes. Daniel nods at them all.

> DANIEL
>
> Morning.

> RICHARD
>
> Daniel, you can start back here on
> the main sheet. That way I can keep
> an eye on you. The rest of you know
> the drill. Let's try and make this two
> wins in a row shall we.

EXT. OCEAN - DAY

Midway out to the race course, Richard runs his crew through the paces as he tries to teach them John's trick.

RICHARD
Prepare to tack! Hold the main!
Daniel, sheet it in more! More! Chad,
hold on -- hold on, now!

Both main and jib go from being slightly backwinded to filling perfectly. The tack couldn't have been more perfect.

RICHARD (CONT'D)
Ease out on the jib! Now ease on
the main! Alright! Now that's how
we tack!

CHAD
I felt like I wanted to release the jib a
lot earlier.

RICHARD
That jib wants to be moving to centre
right at the top of the tack. Watch
till it starts to fill then ease it out and
set it.
We'll follow with the main.
It's all in the timing.

Dean turns to Daniel.

DEAN
Meet Captain Bly. Are you sure
you know what you're getting yourself into?

Daniel shrugs and smiles.

RICHARD

You two, pay attention! You guys
centre the boom as the main loses
power. As soon as Chad sets the jib,
let the rig power up. That way we
accelerate instead of waiting for it to
fill itself. Then you trim.

CANDACE

It wasn't bad though. Let's try
it again.

Nods and waves all around.

RICHARD

Great, here we go. Prepare to tack!

EXT. OCEAN, NEAR THE STARTING LINE - DAY

Daniel is bug-eyed. He doesn't want to screw up. It's exciting. Boats
making close passes. Richard jockeying for the right start position.
Shouting. Finally, seconds before the gun!

RICHARD

Sheet in! Let's race!

EXT. OCEAN - DAY

Into the race, Richard spots Candace up at the bow struggling with
some gear.

> RICHARD
>
> Daniel, could you go give Candace
> a hand. She's going to need help
> getting that chute ready.

> DANIEL
>
> Sure.

Daniel leaves his station and heads forward towards Candace. She's all business as she reaches down inside the sail locker for the spinnaker. Daniel is beside himself as to what to do. Candace is wrestling with something. Suddenly, she sits back up. Pissed right off.

> CANDACE
>
> Shit! Stinking shackle!

(startled by Daniel's presence)

> What are you staring at?

> DANIEL
>
> Mr. Stewart sent me up here to give
> you a hand with the chute.

> CANDACE
>
> I don't need any help, he knows
> better than --

> DANIEL
>
> I think he was hoping you might
> teach me a thing or two about this
> here sail.

                              CANDACE
            Oh, he did?

Just then the bow cuts through a wave. Spray hits Candace and
Daniel. Candace screams at the shock of the cold water. Richard
looks up at the commotion.

                              RICHARD
            Hey! Enough fooling around. Get
            that chute ready. We're coming up to
            the mark.

Candace and Daniel are both dripping wet. The ice is broken. She
points down into the hatch.

                              CANDACE
            Can you reach that top plate and fix
            this shackle and line to it? Damn
            thing's too stiff for me to loosen.

Daniel does as he's instructed. His strong hands easily turn the
shackle. He and Candace ready the sail.

EXT. CHESTER YACHT CLUB – DAY

SUPER: Three weeks later.

James is back, all neat and tidy. The boats are just returning. He
waits impatiently.

The crew is in the middle of a water fight. Candace dumps a pail of
water over Daniel's head. Her laughter fills the air. She sees James
and waves. James points to his watch and holds up his hands as
if to say, "Why so late?" Sadly, the fun fades from Candace's face.

Richard catches Candace's change in expression as he follows her look to shore. He sees James.

EXT. CHESTER YACHT CLUB DOCK – DAY

It's dead calm as Candace hugs James.

> CANDACE
> Sorry, hon. It just died on us out
> there. We almost needed a tow in.
> How was your trip?

James nods at Daniel.

> JAMES
> Who's the new guy?

> CANDACE
> That's Daniel. He's been coming out
> with us. Daddy knows him from
> town. Give me half an hour here to
> get everything stowed away.

> JAMES
> For Christ's sake! Let the others do
> that. I've missed you.

> CANDACE
> James, I can't keep shirking crew
> duties. It's as much a part of sailing
> as the rest.

                    JAMES
        What am I, chopped liver? I've come
        all the way up here to see you, my
        fiancée. Maybe next time I'll just stay
        in Boston.

                    CANDACE
        James, stop it. I'll be up as soon as
        I can. Order me a hot chocolate.
        I'm frozen.

Her loving smile can't crack James. Richard watches James
storm off.

EXT. CHESTER YACHT CLUB - DAY

The boat has been put to bed. Candace finishes hosing down
the deck.

                    RICHARD
        That was a great race today. Time for
        a little celebration. My shout!

Daniel reacts awkwardly, like maybe this is his cue to leave. He
picks up his canvas bag.

                RICHARD (CONT'D)
        You're not going to join us? We're not
        that bad a company, are we?

                    CANDACE
        Besides, since you happened
        along, we've started winning again.

That calls for a celebration, don't
you think?

> CHAD

Come on, Daniel. Live a little.

> DANIEL

Since you put it that way, if you're
the man who pours, I'll certainly be a
friend of yours.

> RICHARD

All right then!

INT. CHESTER YACHT CLUB - DAY

> JAMES

Will you look at this!

James watches as Richard and his crew head up the boardwalk.
James turns to a couple of his snobby friends.

> JAMES (CONT'D)

I am about to have the honour
of drinks with a living, breathing
Cro-Magnon. Are there no rules of
decency left at this club?

EXT. CHESTER YACHT CLUB DECK - DAY

Richard, Daniel, Candace, and James sit at a small table.

DANIEL

... the shed isn't that far from here.
I guess they just chipped away at it
when they could. She'll be a pretty
thing if I ever get her in the water.

James looks bored.

JAMES

Yes, I'm sure it's very special.
Can I get anyone else another drink?

Candace declines. Richard finishes his drink and hands James
his glass.

RICHARD

Scotch, please. Neat, no ice. Thank
you, James. Daniel, would you
like another?

James heads off before Daniel has a chance to respond. He's oblivious to James' attitude.

DANIEL

Maybe I'll tag along. See if there's
any beer. I can't take this hard stuff.

Richard and Candace share a look. She takes the opportunity to
get something off her chest.

CANDACE

All this time I was looking so
forward to seeing James. Why is he
acting like such a jerk?

                    RICHARD
You've finally noticed? His old man
isn't like that! You tell me where he
gets it from?

                    CANDACE
He's been under all this pressure
lately with his exams. I just thought
it was from the stress.

                    RICHARD
Candace, please. Defend him all you
want. He passed his bar exams two
weeks ago. He has no excuse.

Daniel returns with Richard's scotch. Candace looks around.

                    CANDACE
Where's James?

                    DANIEL
Oh, he's talking to some folks by the
bar. Cheers!

Candace doesn't appear all that disappointed. Instead, she turns her
attention to Daniel.

                    CANDACE
What do you do for a living, Daniel?

                    DANIEL
I repair boats at the NSP yards over
in Lunenburg.

RICHARD

Tell us more about this boat
you inherited.

Daniel shyly takes a sip from his beer. He isn't used to being the focus of attention.

DANIEL

My granddad and father started
building her back before the war. My
plan is to finish her.

CANDACE

All by yourself? I wouldn't know
where to start! Would you, Daddy?

Suddenly, James reappears.

JAMES

Candace, dearest, there are some
friends I'd like you to meet.

He points back to his friends across the room. Candace gives Daniel an apologetic look.

CANDACE

Please, excuse us. Daniel. It was nice
talking to you.

Daniel starts to respond, but James has already dragged Candace out of earshot.

James pulls Candace close.

JAMES

Darling, you're too polite! That
pathetic little man was putting me to
sleep. Watching the ice melt in my
drink was more interesting.

Daniel watches them for a moment and then turns back to Richard,
who smiles.

RICHARD

Don't worry. He's only here till
Friday. Come on, we should join the
rest of our crew.

EXT. CHESTER YACHT CLUB — EARLY MORNING

Daniel waits in the parking lot with his canvas bag. It's unusu-
ally quiet for a weekend. Normally, the parking lot would be full.
Richard's car pulls in. Daniel gets up and dusts himself off as he
approaches the driver's side window.

DANIEL

Morning! I was starting to wonder if
anyone was going to show today.

RICHARD

There's no racing this weekend.
I'm sorry; I had no way of letting
you know.

CANDACE

You need to get a phone!

DANIEL

There's an idea. Okay. No worries.
I guess I can go back to sleep then.
What about next weekend?

RICHARD

Same time, same place. Awfully sorry
about today though.

Daniel heads back towards his truck. Richard looks at Candace.
His eyes say, "Invite him if you want." Candace leans across her
father and calls out the window.

CANDACE

Daniel, why don't you come out with
Daddy and me? It won't be racing,
but it will still be practice for you.

Daniel looks at Richard, then back to Candace.

DANIEL

I don't want to impose.
Thanks anyway.

Daniel turns to leave again. Candace gives her father a nudge along
with her best "It was your idea" look.

RICHARD

Yes, sailing doesn't have to be
all serious. It can have its relax-
ing moments.

Daniel smiles back, unaware of their subtleties.

Dean Eilertson

                    DANIEL
        You're sure? I don't want to be in the
        way or anything.

EXT. OCEAN – DAY

Daniel stares up at the rigging.

                    DANIEL
        It sure isn't as tense when we're
        not racing.

Richard sits at the helm lost in thought. Daniel fidgets. Candace
appears from below deck with a plate of sandwiches. The focus
turns to food. She serves Daniel first.

                    CANDACE
        That boat you inherited, the one
        you mentioned at the club the other
        night, what class is it?

                    DANIEL
        It's a Roué. She's a forty-three-foot
        single-masted sloop.

                    CANDACE
        A Roué? What's that?
        Someone's name?

Richard perks up, taking interest in what he is hearing.

RICHARD

Roué was a boat designer from these parts, years ago, starting back in the early twenties.

DANIEL

That's right. He designed the Bluenose schooner that John used to race on.

RICHARD

John raced on the Bluenose?

DANIEL

Way back when they used to have those IFR races. I think they even won a few.

CANDACE

IFR?

DANIEL

International Fishermen's Race.

RICHARD

That would make John quite the modest man. They only held the cup for twenty years! God, what a gorgeous boat. You've seen her, Candace, two summers ago, she was at the museum in Lunenburg.

Candace is impressed.

                    DANIEL

My grandfather hired Bill Roué to
draw up the plans. I'm working off
his drawings I found in the shed.

                    RICHARD

Daniel, it sounds like you might have
a real gem on your hands, a classic.

                    CANDACE

That's incredible. I can hardly wait to
see it.

                    RICHARD

How long before she's in the water?

                    DANIEL

I'm hoping to get her in the water by
next spring. She'll need a mast and
rigging after that.

                    CANDACE

That's so amazing. You're actually
building your own sailboat.

Richard watches his daughter's interest in Daniel's adventure. He
smiles to himself as he looks out to sea.

EXT. RICHARD'S YACHT - DAY

Richard sits at the helm watching Candace and Daniel up at the
bow getting lines ready to hoist the spinnaker.

CANDACE

You go back and fly it. I'll set the
pole. We're ready, Daddy!

Daniel heads back to the cockpit and gets the spinnaker halyard set
up around a winch. He braces and watches, waiting for Richard to
give him his cue.

RICHARD

You two ready? We'll jibe at the bell
buoy. Candace, brace yourself!

They near the buoy, its bell clanging. It's beam to beam with Richard.

RICHARD (CONT'D)

Prepare to jibe!

Daniel pulls in on the halyard, the spinnaker rises skyward. Candace
feeds it out from its forward hatch. The wind fills the chute with
all its colours, perfectly. Candace sets the pole like the skilled sailor
that she is. Richard looks at his daughter laughing and having fun.
He loves these times. He loves his daughter deeply.

EXT. TANNER BOATHOUSE – DAY

A grey foggy, rainy day. A woman's hand knocks on the door.

CANDACE

Hello, is anybody there? Daniel?

INT. TANNER BOAT SHED – DAY

From below deck, Daniel's head pops up. Did he hear something?

CANDACE (O.S.)
Hello! It's Candace. I've come to see
your boat.

DANIEL
Candace?! Come in! The doors open!

Candace enters carrying an open umbrella. She takes a moment for
her eyes to adjust. It's the first time he's seen her without her bulky
sailing gear. She looks like she could be a New York model, wearing
just a touch of makeup, in her khaki shorts and a rugby sweater.

CANDACE
I hope I'm not disturbing you?

Daniel swings down from the bracing that supports the hull.

DANIEL
No, not at all, sure wish this rain
would go away though.

CANDACE
Me too. I was supposed to go on a
picnic today.

DANIEL
It still might clear up.

CANDACE
I was driving by and saw
your pick-up.

Daniel is shell-shocked by Candace's good looks and surprise visit.

CANDACE (CONT'D)
Wow! So, this is your boat!?

DANIEL
This is she, big old beast with a ton
more work still to do.
Meet Dreammaker. . .

Candace looks around at the shed as she warms herself by the
wood stove. The double doors are open. A fishing boat makes its
way through the fog. The plans are rolled out on a small table. A
dirty coffee mug keeps the loose papers from blowing away.

CANDACE
This is so amazing, Daniel. I can't
believe this space. Do you live here?

DANIEL
Every chance I get. There's so much
work yet to do on -- you mean
"live" live?

CANDACE
Yes.

DANIEL
This is just temporary. I rented my
place out for the summer to get some
extra cash. I stay here so I can get
more work done on the boat.

CANDACE

This could be a sculptor's studio.
Look at your view. I'd kill to have
this space.

DANIEL

You're an artist?

CANDACE

A wannabe. I'm studying fine arts
at home in Boston. Sculpting and
painting major.

DANIEL

Well, you're welcome to fix this place
up, if I can ever get this boat done
and out of here.

CANDACE

In my dreams!

Candace takes a moment to look at Daniel. Torn jeans, faded singlet, hair tied back, blue eyes, strong tanned arms.

CANDACE (CONT'D)

So, are you going to show me
your boat?

DANIEL

Sure. Come over here. There's
a ladder.

Daniel watches Candace climb as he braces the ladder. She's all smiles, so pleased to be there. Daniel holds the ladder, the view from his angle looking very good.

                    CANDACE
          Daniel, this is gorgeous! I had no
          idea. This is amazing. Wow!

She descends into the cabin area. Daniel is still a bit stunned by her beauty.

                    DANIEL
          Uh, yeah, thanks. Glad you like it.

(to himself)

          Wow! God give me strength!

INT. DREAMMAKER — DAY

Candace takes in the space.

                    CANDACE
          Your galley area? It's a nice size.

Daniel remains shy and nervous.

                    DANIEL
          Forward there, that's the -- sleeping
          quarters and storage for the sails.

                    CANDACE
        You'll have lots of room for both. This
        wood is going to look amazing once
        it's varnished.

She's finally picking up on Daniel's nervousness.

                CANDACE (CONT'D)
        I'm not disturbing you, am I? You're
        acting kind of funny.

                     DANIEL
        I guess I'm just not used to visitors
        is all.

Awkward pause. Candace's face brightens with an idea.

                    CANDACE
        How about lunch? I'll go get my
        picnic stuff.

INT. TANNER BOAT SHED — MINUTES LATER

Candace has laid out a checkered tablecloth and her picnic food.
Daniel finishes putting more wood in the stove.

                    CANDACE
        I can't get over this place. It should be
        part museum. You could frame some
        of these drawings. Look here, they're
        signed originals.

Daniel nods as he looks but pays no mind, unable to appreciate
how remarkable his life is. He points at the drawing.

DANIEL

See here? The ballast in the keel. I've
shifted that back some to help her
cut through the waves easier.

CANDACE

If you shift it back, won't you ride
up the wave instead of cutting
through it?

DANIEL

That's what I thought, but this is a
full keel design. Nowadays you want
the weight evenly distributed but
over a shorter distance, so it doesn't
seesaw as much.

CANDACE

Right under the mainsail with its
force back of the mast. Who taught
you all this?

DANIEL

John. He's figured out all kinds
of tricks to make these old boats
go faster.

Candace smirks.

DANIEL (CONT'D)

What are you grinning at? You think
I'm making this up?

CANDACE

No! This kind of thing people
usually only dream about or write
books about doing. You're doing
it for real. I wouldn't have the first
clue where to begin. The whole idea
is overwhelming.

DANIEL

The thing I find funny is, here I am
building a sailboat, and I don't know
the first thing about sailing.

CANDACE

And then there's me. I can sail but
don't know the first thing about
building boats. How about I make
you a deal?

DANIEL

Oh yeah?

CANDACE

I'll teach you all I know about sailing,
and you teach me about boat building. I can be your apprentice. That
would be fair, wouldn't it?

Daniel laughs.

DANIEL

I suppose.

CANDACE

What? You don't think I can work?
Feel these arms, buddy!

DANIEL

No, it's not that at all. Really! I'm
kinda more -- I don't know, it's weird.

CANDACE

Weird?

DANIEL

Why anyone would want to spend
time working on this boat in
this mess if they didn't have to is
beyond me.

CANDACE

Right. It's so terrible here. Building a
boat, learning how to use tools, being
taught by an expert boat builder.

DANIEL

Expert?

CANDACE

According to my dad, you can do no
wrong. He thinks you're amazing.

DANIEL

Really! Your father said that?

CANDACE

Yes. If James hears one more thing
about how great you are or how well
the boat is performing with you on
our crew, he's going to spit.

DANIEL

Your father really thinks I'm
doing okay?

CANDACE

We all do. You're a natural.

DANIEL

Come on, who's making fun now?

CANDACE

Trust me.

DANIEL

What about Boston? Do you think
he'll let me crew along?

CANDACE

That's months away. We haven't even
qualified yet.

DANIEL

We'll qualify. We're kickin' butt.
What are we now, three for four?

CANDACE

"Kicking butt?"

DANIEL

Sorry, I shouldn't talk like that,
should I?

CANDACE

You must think I'm a real prude.
Well, I'm not. I've just never heard it
called that before, that's all.

EXT. OCEAN - DAY

Another weekend race is underway. Richard, Candace, Daniel, and
Chad work hard at their stations.

EXT. OCEAN - DAY

Midway through the race, Richard is at the helm. They are in the
lead. Spray washes over the deck, soaking Daniel. Chad and Dean
man their winches. Candace is focused on the sails. One can't
imagine anything more beautiful or thrilling than sailing a classic
yacht while out in the lead.

INT. TANNER BOAT SHED - NIGHT

Daniel eats some soup. His gear hangs everywhere drying. John has
dropped by for a visit.

JOHN GREEK

I was startin' to think we'd lost ya.
Haven't seen ya. 'cept for work, you've
become quite the stranger.

DANIEL

It's all this sailing. Takes up a lot of
time. You must know how it is. The
only time I got left is spent sleeping
or here on the boat.

JOHN GREEK

(chuckles)
I remember when ya first got
down here, you was afraid that the
small-town pace was goin' ta drive
you crazy.

DANIEL

Yeah, who would have thought
I'd turn into a yacht racer? Thanks
to you!

JOHN GREEK

So, tell me, is it really the sailing that
keeps you goin' back for more, or is
it the daughter? I've see her parked
here a fair bit.

DANIEL

We've got an arrangement... She
teaches me about sailing, and I show
her how to build boats. That's all.

JOHN GREEK

Something tells me there's more to
this yarn than what you're spinnin'.

DANIEL

John, she's engaged. Her fiancé
is loaded. She lives in some huge
house in Boston. All that girl wants
is to learn 'bout boat buildin'. If for
some reason we should stay friends,
that's more than I could have
ever imagined.

JOHN GREEK

I may be old, but I'm not blind. I
think she likes you. Women look for
more out of life than fancy houses
ya know.

DANIEL

Who are you tryin' ta kid? You should
see these people. They got their cars
and fancy boats and big houses and
their yachting gloves and shit. What
have I got?

JOHN GREEK

Well, I got eyes, an' I say she likes ya.
Now, we going drinking or not?

DANIEL

Come on, I'll buy the first round.

John throws Daniel his coat. Daniel hits the lights.

INT. JOHN'S PICK-UP - NIGHT

John and Daniel head towards town. They're talking and laughing, an oncoming cars' headlights illuminate their faces.

INT. JAMES' CAR – NIGHT

James and Candace are midway into a conversation.

> CANDACE
> James, this is a part of what being together is about. For better or for worse, right?

> JAMES
> So, what about this little cod-cleaning friend of yours? What's going on there?

> CANDACE
> He's teaching me about boat build-ing. I teach him about sailing, and that's all!

> JAMES
> Oh! That's nice. You're going to sit there and tell me that besides playing sailor, this moron can build boats too? How gullible do you think I am?

> CANDACE
> You're the moron!

James attempts to ease the situation. He knows the right buttons to push. A 180-degree emotional turnaround.

                           JAMES
                    Okay, I'm sorry, pumpkin.

                           CANDACE
                    I am so completely disappointed in
                    you, James.

                           JAMES
                    Why? Because I can't bond with your
                    father? Come on. You've got to help
                    me out here.

                           CANDACE
                    Come back on the boat, come sailing
                    with us.

                           JAMES
                    Oh, that would really help.
                    Remember what happened the
                    last time?

He laughs and shakes his head.

                           CANDACE
                    Trust me. If you got out there and
                    really tried, you'd make so many
                    points with him.

EXT. CHESTER YACHT CLUB PARKING LOT - MORNING

James drives up with Candace in the passenger seat. Daniel stands
waiting down on the dock by the boat. He waves.

INT. JAMES' CAR — MORNING

James gestures towards Daniel.

> JAMES
> What's cod boy doing here?

> CANDACE
> James! Daniel is part of our crew.

EXT. CHESTER YACHT CLUB DOCK — MORNING

Daniel greets Candace as she climbs aboard with James.

> DANIEL
> Morning! Looks like the wind is
> finally starting to pick up.

> CANDACE
> Morning, Daniel. You remember
> James. Here, honey, I'll stow our
> stuff below.

Candace takes James' bag and disappears below deck.

Daniel is still standing on the dock as he reaches out for James' hand, but James doesn't reciprocate. As Daniel goes to climb aboard James taps him on the shoulder. With no one else around to witness, James seizes his chance.

> JAMES
> Not today, Danny boy. No room! You
> need to sit this one out.

> DANIEL
> No room? Or not welcome?

JAMES

You're the smart one. You figure it
out. Now run along.

James waves Daniel off like he's dealing with some sort of sub-
human species. He then turns and disappears below deck.

EXT. CHESTER YACHT CLUB PARKING LOT - MORNING

In a rage, Daniel throws his stuff into the back of his truck and
gets inside. He turns the key. The engine turns over but won't
start. Again!

DANIEL

Come on!

He pumps the gas pedal! Turns the key again.

INT. GALLEY — MORNING

Candace finishes putting James' gear way.

CANDACE

James, could you hand me
Daniel's bag.

JAMES

Turns out Danny won't be joining us
today. He's decided his time would
be better spent watching us win
from shore.

Candace glares at him.

CANDACE

What did you say to him?

She pushes past James and races up onto the deck.

EXT. RICHARD'S YACHT - MORNING

Candace comes up above deck just as Daniel's truck finally starts, belching exhaust. The back-up lights come on.

INT. DANIEL'S TRUCK - MORNING

In Daniel's rear view mirror, Candace waves both arms. Daniel pulls away, oblivious.

Chad and Dean pass Daniel going the other way.

INT. DEAN AND CHAD'S CAR — MORNING

Chad cranks his head around as Daniel roars past.

CHAD

Where's he going?

DEAN

Must have forgotten something.

CHAD

We're running late as it is. He'd better step on it.

EXT. CHESTER YACHT CLUB DOCK - MORNING

At the boat, Richard is pacing.

                    RICHARD
          You say you saw him earlier? We
          can't wait any longer. Damn it! James,
          I guess you're the man on deck
          today. Candace, can I talk to you for
          a second?

Candace heads back to the cockpit. James catches the looks from
Chad and Dean and tries to change the subject.

                     JAMES
          You heard the captain. Dean, you get
          the dock lines.

                    RICHARD
          Below, dear. Chad, Dean, get us ready.
          Let's go!

EXT. TANNER BOAT SHED - DAY

Daniel steps outside, smoke drifts up from the chimney.

EXT. OCEAN - DAY

Yachts race out in the bay. Richard's boat is back in third position. Candace looks towards shore. She sees Daniel walking back
towards his shed, pouring out what's left of his coffee as he goes.
He pulls the shed's double doors closed.

                     JAMES
          I still think we can catch them if we
          head more into shore. That's a nice
          breeze over there, isn't it?

                    CHAD
          (under his breath to Dean)
          No, that's the tide washing over
          rocks. Idiot!

                    DEAN
          Where does he get off pretending he
          can sail?

                    CHAD
          Just stay clear of your dad when we
          get back to shore.

Candace sits with James, their legs hanging over the windward rail.
She's nervous.

                  CANDACE
          Coffee, Daddy?

                  RICHARD
          No thanks, dear. I'd rather just
          savour this moment without. Thank
          you though.

He gives her a fake smile.

INT. HARDWARE STORE - DAY

Daniel is picking up supplies for his boat when Chad and
Dean enter.

                    DEAN
          Where the hell did you disappear to
          on Sunday?

DANIEL

I couldn't make it. I'm sorry. I should
have phoned or somethin'.

CHAD

Bullshit. We passed you on the road.
You were coming from the club.

Daniel tries to change the subject.

DANIEL

So, how'd you guys do?

DEAN

Thanks to Sir James, we got blown
out of the water.

CHAD

Yeah, but it was almost worth it
to watch Richard tear a huge strip
off James for pulling another of
his stunts.

DANIEL

Candace must be really pissed at
your father.

DEAN

She'll get over it. What she sees in
the guy, I'll never know. He's no
sailor, that's for sure!

CHAD

You've got to feel sorry for her
though. She's the one marrying
the jerk.

DEAN

What about me? You think she's got
problems? I'm going to get him as
a brother-in-law!

CHAD

Our problem now is qualifying.
Lucky for us, James heads back to
Boston tomorrow.

DANIEL

We have to win four straight now.
That's going to be tough to pull off.

CHAD

That's the spirit, man, "we" being the
operative word here. Just make sure
you get your ass there for Saturday.

DANIEL

Thanks, guys. I suppose it's balls to
the walls now, hey?

A couple of slaps on the back as Chad and Dean exit.

Daniel picks out a pair of sailing gloves then heads towards the
cashier with the rest of his hardware.

EXT. CHESTER YACHT CLUB — EARLY MORNING

Daniel walks down the dock towards Richard. He fools Daniel
with a hello and then slugs him in the arm.

> RICHARD
> Where the hell were you
> last weekend?

Daniel rubs his sore arm. Richard is rightly pissed off.

> DANIEL
> That's a fine hello. Look, I'm sorry --

> RICHARD
> Daniel, I'm not ticked at you for
> missing the race. I'm more upset
> that you would let a guy like James
> treat you that way. You are a part of
> this crew. You've earned your spot,
> and no one has the right to take that
> away, okay?

> DANIEL
> I just thought I was doin' the
> right thing.

> RICHARD
> Well, you didn't! Instead, you let a
> bunch of your friends down. So, no
> more Mr. Nice Guy. Got it?

EXT. RICHARD'S YACHT — MORNING

Chad admires Daniel's new purchase.

                    CHAD
          Nice gloves! This must mean you're
          finally getting serious.

Daniel laughs.

                    DANIEL
          Knock it off. Permission to
          come aboard?

Dean extends his hand.

                    DEAN
          Get up here!

EXT. OCEAN - DAY

Heading out to the race course, Richard checks the main shrouds
with his wire-tension gauge. It looks sort of like a handheld scale
for weighing fish.

                    RICHARD
          Why are these shrouds cranked way
          up again? Look at this. This one's at
          eighty-five, and the other one is at
          seventy! I had them set at fifty. Why
          did we change them, guys?

                    CANDACE
          James thought they were too slack.
          He said we should be running with
          more pre-bend in the mast.

CHAD

And I disagreed. I told him you said
a slacker rig would be better in these
light downwind legs. But he went
and did it anyway.

Candace listens while trying to hold back the tears welling up in
her eyes.

RICHARD

Hon, seriously, it's no big deal. We'll
just set them back.

Candace pushes past him and heads below deck. Richard sees the
boys looking at him.

RICHARD (CONT'D)

Daniel, set them back to fifty please.
Dean, get those fenders in! Chad,
take us out. Thanks, guys. I'll be up in
a minute.

Richard heads below after Candace.

INT. GALLEY - MORNING

Richard pours himself a coffee. Candace appears, red-eyed.

RICHARD

You must know I'm not happy with
the way James treated Daniel. And
now I find out he's been messing
with my boat?

CANDACE

I know, I get it. Anyways, I'm not
crying because of that.

RICHARD

What is it then?

CANDACE

I'm just really confused right now.
Okay? I don't appreciate what James
did to Daniel any more than you do.
These last few months have really
made me start to question if he's the
kind of man I should be marrying.
Just a lot on my mind. . .

RICHARD

Don't get me wrong, James is basi-
cally a good man. I'd say he has some
growing up to do, but the good side
is you've still got a long time between
now and your wedding.

CANDACE

Right now -- I need to be doing
more of what I enjoy, and James
needs to use this time to grow up.
I just hope this last stunt will make
him think twice about doing what he
did ever again.

RICHARD

So, we're okay?

Candace gives her father a big hug.

>>> CANDACE
>>> Thanks, Dad. Now let's go kick
>>> some butt.

She laughs through her tears and stuffed nose. Richard gives Candace a spank through all her sailing gear. She exits, laughing.

>>> RICHARD
>>> You watch your language, young lady!

INT. TANNER BOAT SHED - SUNSET

Daniel is splicing a new jib sheet for Richard's boat. The double doors are open. Candace appears wearing a cotton summer dress. She looks more beautiful than ever.

>>> CANDACE
>>> Do you ever stop working?

Daniel looks up in surprise.

>>> DANIEL
>>> You trying to give me a heart attack?
>>> I'm just finishing this for your dad.
>>> Good race today, hey?

>>> CANDACE
>>> Daniel, I wanted to come by and
>>> apologize in person. I don't know
>>> what James said, but he had no
>>> right making you feel like you
>>> didn't belong.

                    DANIEL

No worries. I had other things to
do anyway. He can take my spot
any time he wants. If there's room, I
crew. If not, I go away. That's always
been understood.

                    CANDACE

Well, that's not going to happen.
James left today. He's gone back to
Boston for the rest of the summer.
Besides, I was missing the work here
on your boat.

                    DANIEL

Is that why I haven't seen you
all week?

                    CANDACE

I was wondering if you would notice.

Candace steps up to Daniel and looks him in the eyes. She puts her
arms around him and gives him a long hug, her eyes closed. She
kisses him on the cheek, runs her hands lightly down his arms, and
looks into his eyes.

                CANDACE (CONT'D)
         Are we still friends?

Daniel stares at her in astonishment. His hands go to hug her back
but stop. His smile reveals his attraction for her.

                    DANIEL

Yeah, I suppose.

CANDACE

Suppose? Yes or no? I don't want to
hear about this later.

DANIEL

Yes!

With that she turns and heads upstairs to Daniel's sleeping loft,
pulling a pair of jeans and a T-shirt off a clothesline as she goes. At
the top of the stairs, she pulls a curtain closed for privacy.

CANDACE

That's better. Now put me to work.

INT. TANNER BOAT SHED - NIGHT

Few women look even better in a pair of jeans and a T-shirt.
Candace nods as Daniel explains what he's doing. As he works,
she stares at him and smiles. Something is definitely happening,
chemically speaking.

DANIEL

Ouch!

He shakes his hand madly.

CANDACE

What happened?

DANIEL

This fir lumber is full of slivers. Got
myself a good one this time.

CANDACE

Let me see. Do you have any first-
aid stuff?

Candace steadies Daniel's hand against her leg as she works the
sliver out with a needle. Success! Candace proudly shows off the
sliver. Then she carefully bandages Daniel's hand. As she works, he
looks at her hair, her face, her smile.

A pregnant pause as Candace adjusts, moves closer to Daniel. They
kiss. They stop. They laugh nervously. Daniel hesitates, not knowing
if he is allowed to kiss her again. Candace pushes Daniel back into
a soft pile of canvas tarps. Candace falls on top of him, looking into
his eyes. With a mischievous look, she starts tickling him.

CANDACE

Take that, Mr. Boat Builder!

With out-of-control giggles, in defense Daniel pulls a piece of
canvas over Candace and starts tickling her back.

EXT. OCEAN - DAY

The main sail's boom swings past as they complete a tack. Mid-
race, Richard's boat is in second place.

RICHARD

Come on, we've got one last chance!
This is our windward leg! Daniel!

DANIEL

What?

RICHARD

What do you figure, lad? Can we get
any more speed out of this tub?

DANIEL

Hard to say. She feels like
she's stalling.

RICHARD

Look at how much the top of the
main is twisting off. We're losing a
lot of power.

DANIEL

I'm sheeted in as far as I can. Why
can't the mainsail hold its shape?

RICHARD

Feels like we're right on that edge.
What are we blowing, fifteen to
twenty knots?

DANIEL

Twenty at least! We're flying! Can we
flatten the main by sheeting in on the
swinging backstay?

RICHARD

Now you're thinking! Dial it up three
turns. Dean! Take in the outhaul.
Chad on winch, close up the jib six to
eight inches.

                    DANIEL
Don't worry. Someday I'll get all this.
We're here to win or nothing, right?

                    RICHARD
That's right! Chad, more in on the
jib sheet! Candace, help him. Dean,
one last tug on the outhaul. Daniel,
ease out on the main sheet. Let's kick
some butt!

The crew lets out a howl. Daniel looks around at the team!

The top of the main sail flattens as the hull speed increases. The
crew of the leading yacht watch as their lead slips away. Richard's
yacht inches ahead. Coming up to the last mark, the two boats are
now beam to beam. Richard calls it. He legally now has the right
of way.

              RICHARD (CONT'D)
Starboard!

                    CHAD
Chute's ready!

                  CANDACE
Up haul ready!

                  RICHARD
Now! Tacking!

They're functioning like a well-oiled machine. Dean and Candace
wrestle to stow the jib. The main refills, as does the spinnaker. They
round the mark in the lead by half a boat length. Everyone cheers.

RICHARD (CONT'D)
Let's take it home! Yahoo!

It's a close race. They cross the finish line in first place by such a fine margin.

RICHARD (CONT'D)
Great work! That was anyone's race
though. Wow!

He gives Daniel a wink and a thumbs-up.

RICHARD (CONT'D)
Good job, guys.

INT. CHESTER YACHT CLUB - DAY

Daniel is busy scribbling out some calculations on a piece of paper.

DANIEL
We should take her out during the
week for a real tune up.

RICHARD
One thing I'd like to check again
are those new bushings we put
in the rudder. After what we saw
happen today, we're still losing
time somewhere.

Candace sits with them listening to every word.

                    CANDACE
         Let's take it out right now. It's light
         till nine.

                    RICHARD
         You know where it's parked.

He gets up and signs the bar tab.

                RICHARD (CONT'D)
         Drop by later. You can fill me in
         on what you find. You two feel like
         steaks tonight?

He exits before they can answer, assuming it's a "yes."

                    DANIEL
         Is he serious?

                    CANDACE
         Yeah! Come on.

She gets up and heads towards the door.

Daniel sits a second longer. Downs his lemonade. Gets up and
looks around, then follows Candace. He can't believe they're going
out on their own!

EXT. RICHARD'S YACHT - DAY

Candace is at the helm. Daniel is lying on his back sighting up the
mast. All business.

DANIEL

I don't know. Things look alright to
me. Try tacking, and let's see what
she does.

Daniel watches the boom cross over as the sail resets.

DANIEL (CONT'D)

A new set of battens might help.
Three and five are looking a little
wonky. Do you have a bosun's
harness aboard?

CANDACE

Yeah, it's down below. What's
the plan?

DANIEL

We might as well do a visual of the
full mast. You can use the main sheet
winch to take me up.

CANDACE

I want to go up! I trust you more
than myself with winches.

EXT. RICHARD'S YACHT – MINUTES LATER

The sails are down. The boat is at anchor. Daniel is tying Candace
into the bosun's harness.

DANIEL

Okay, step through these leg loops.
Ok now this belt. (Daniel has to

reach around Candace, sort of
like hugging)

You want these leg loops pretty tight.
Otherwise it, uh, rides up.
Put your weight into it.

Candace is all smiles as he works away. She sits and immediately starts to swing out and away from Daniel. She lets out a squeal and grabs Daniel by his arm.

> DANIEL (CONT'D)
> Sorry. You alright?

Candace gives him a tickle, then a quick kiss.

> CANDACE
> I'm fine. Take me up.

At the winch, Daniel eases Candace up to the top of the mast, 55 feet in the air. Candace takes in the view.

> CANDACE (CONT'D)
> It's so amazing up here! I can see
> for miles.

> DANIEL
> I thought you said you'd been up
> there before.

> CANDACE
> I lied!

Candace spots something below the water's surface right under the boat.

> CANDACE (CONT'D)
> I think I see our problem. Looks
> like a piece of net is wrapped around
> our keel.

> DANIEL
> Great! These guys hate it when we
> tear up their nets.

> CANDACE
> Don't they realize that we have these
> races! Why do they even set them
> out here?

> DANIEL
> These guys are trying to make a
> living. They could care less about your
> races. I just hope it's not tangled in
> our prop.

> CANDACE
> Our races! You said 'your races'.

> DANIEL
> These nets are worth a fortune. We
> need to try and save it. I'm bringing
> you down. Where's that swim-
> ming mask?

Daniel lowers Candace and then readies himself for the task at hand.

> CANDACE
> You're not going into that freezing
> water, are you?

> DANIEL
> It's summer, ain't it! This water won't
> be getting' any warmer.

EXT. UNDERWATER - DAY

Daniel dives in with a length of rope. He ties it to the net, then goes to work trying to loosen the tangled mess. He heads up for air.

EXT. OCEAN – DAY

Daniel bobs in the waves.

> DANIEL
> Cleat this quick before it gets away!
> Wow! That's cold.

He takes another breath and then dives back down to the keel.

EXT. UNDERWATER - DAY

A couple more pushes, and the net starts to slide off the keel as it sinks.

EXT. RICHARD'S YACHT – DAY

The rope pays out and then goes taut. Daniel climbs aboard, shivering, not quite hypothermic.

                    CANDACE
          Your lips are blue!

She puts her hand on his chest.

                    CANDACE (CONT'D)
          You're frozen!

She rubs his back vigorously.

                    DANIEL
          I-I'll — b-be — o-k-kay -- in --
          a m-m-minute.

                    CANDACE
          They say the best first aid is to get
          under some blankets with someone
          who's warm.

Daniel gives her a look of bewilderment and disbelief. Candace
howls with laughter.

                    CANDACE (CONT'D)
          God, you make some of the funni-
          est faces!

                    DANIEL
          A-and y-y-ou m-ma-ke t-the fun-n-
          niest jokes!

                    CANDACE
          Daniel, you know I'd do whatever
          it took to warm you up if you really
          needed saving.

She throws him a towel.

> DANIEL
> Y-you ke-e-ep that up, a-and I'm
> going b-back in!

> CANDACE
> Don't you dare!

Daniel's strong back and arms as he pulls up the net.

> CANDACE (CONT'D)
> God, where did you get
> those muscles?

> DANIEL
> What now?

> CANDACE
> These!
> (puts her hands around his biceps)
> You're sooo -- strong.

Daniel is shy, but he doesn't mind the attention.

> DANIEL
> I work, girl. That's what workin' in a
> boatyard does for ya.

Daniel sees a painted yellow-and-red marker on the net. All
Candace sees is Daniel.

DANIEL (CONT'D)
This belongs to Donny Gullett.
He's going to be real happy to get
this back.

EXT. RICHARD'S YACHT - DAY

As they motor back, the net lies on the deck. Daniel is at the helm. Candace joins him. Between sips of hot tea, they exchange looks. Candace moves closer. It's a bit breezy. She puts his arm around her for comfort and warmth. Candace looks at Daniel with total sincerity.

CANDACE
Daniel, I had such a great afternoon.

The look she gives Daniel followed by her snuggles says it all.

INT. THE STEWARTS' HOUSE — EVENING

Dean greets Candace at the door as she enters.

DEAN
Where's Daniel? I thought he was
coming for dinner.

CANDACE
He'll be here in a while. We had a
net wrapped around the keel. Daniel's
returning it to the owner.

Richard enters and gives Candace a hug.

RICHARD

Where's Daniel? You scare him off?

DEAN

Yeah, after he ran your boat aground,
he dove off and swam to shore.

RICHARD

That's a wise man.

CANDACE

Daddy!

RICHARD

Everything okay though? Boat
checked out?

CANDACE

I was up in the bosun's harness and
saw this net all tangled up around the
keel. Daniel had to dive in and got
it off.

RICHARD

That would be enough to slow
anyone down. What were you doing
in the bosun's harness?

CANDACE

We did a check on the whole mast,
that's when I saw the net. He had me
on the winch. We were fine. Actually,
it was a riot.

                        RICHARD
          So, you had fun? A few laughs?

                        CANDACE
          Daddy, Daniel was a perfect gentle-
          man. We're just good friends, and
          that's all.

                        RICHARD
          Hey, I just asked if you had a few
          laughs. If you're feeling a little guilty
          about spending a nice afternoon with
          some good-looking single guy, hey,
          that's not my problem!

                        CANDACE
          (blushing)
          We worked. We checked every-
          thing over.

                         DEAN
          Ya. More like you checked each
          other over.

                        RICHARD
          Dean, that's enough. Get cleaned up.
          Dinner should be in half an hour.

EXT. NSP REPAIR YARD - DAY

Josef confronts Daniel.

JOSEF SORENSEN

Time off? Dis here is our busiest
time of year. We got work ta do here!
You get what I'm sayin'?

DANIEL

I've worked real hard for this
chance, Joe. If we win this next race,
I'm going to need more than the
weekend for this Halifax/Boston
race. Then that's it for the year. If I
can't go, Richard will have to find
someone to take my place.

JOSEF SORENSEN

You tink I give two hoots? Your work
an' future is steady here.
Jus' forget 'bout dis sailing bullshit.
Enough with the games already!

DANIEL

All I'm asking for is the Monday. I'll
catch the bus back and be here for
Tuesday morning. Come on, Joe, it's
just the one day.

Josef shakes his head. He's just about had enough.

JOSEF SORENSEN

Monday! Den dat's it! You do dat
race, and den it's back to work!
Hundred percent!

                          DANIEL
Fair enough. Thanks, Joe. This means
a lot.

                     JOSEF SORENSEN
Jus' make sure ya win. Few a da boys
got money riding on yar boat. A-an'
I want ya to show those other Polly
Wogs what a fella from here's got!

Josef tries to say it with sternness which then breaks into a smile.

EXT. CHESTER YACHT CLUB - NIGHT

Richard and the crew celebrate. They've just won their last race.
They're going to Boston!

EXT. LUNENBURG HARBOUR - DAY

SUPER: Halifax/Boston race day.

The starting line is surrounded by a flotilla of local well-wishers
and committee boats. The 10-minute flag is run up the mast of the
main committee boat.

Officials on shore ready the starting cannon. Daniel's friends from
work are there to cheer on their local boy. The entire atmosphere is
very festive.

The 10-minute flag drops, the competitors start jockeying their
boats for their start line positions. Finally, the cord to the start cannon's firing system is jerked back, and the cannon belches flame
as it roars. The race is on! Fog horns and clanging bells on board

the flotilla of boats combined with cheers from the onlookers fill the air.

EXT. NSP REPAIR YARD - DAY

John turns to Josef.

> JOHN GREEK
> I really don't like the look of this
> weather moving in.

> JOSEF SORENSEN
> She don't look so good, does she?
> Day might outrun it dough. D-hose
> boats are a hell of lot faster den what
> we used to run.

> JOHN GREEK
> Josef my friend, I hope you're right.

EXT. LUNENBURG HARBOUR - DAY

The sailboats head out to sea. To the north a system of scary dark ominous clouds. To the south it still looks fairly calm, just a bit of blue sky with some none threating, fluffy clouds.

EXT. RICHARD'S YACHT – LATE EVENING

The seas are running with huge whitecapped waves. The skies are black. Not a star in the sky. It's pouring rain. The icy black Atlantic sprays up over the bow in torrents. This has turned into some big, serious weather.

RICHARD

Prepare to change over to the storm
jib. We need to get a double reef
in the main. Dean! Daniel! All
hands ondeck! This weather is going
for shit!

CHAD

Candace! Make sure you are hooked
into the jackline!

Candace checks her lifeline and shows it to Chad.

CANDACE

You don't think we can outrun this?

CHAD

We've been trying! We're deep in
it now!

Richard eyes a freak wave off the port side.

RICHARD

Hang on!

BOOM! Like an explosion, the seas send Richard's boat for a knockdown. It's a blur of figures in rain gear and water. Total confusion!
Massive waves wash over the deck, sending everything crashing.

INT. RICHARD'S YACHT - DAY

Daniel and Dean have been trying to rest up for their night watch.
They are both wide awake now, after hearing Richard's orders. All
hell is breaking lose. Daniel struggles to pull on his rain gear. Water

pours in down the companionway steps. Dean, who was in a higher bunk, has been thrown into a bulkhead. He's hurt!

EXT. RICHARD'S YACHT - DAY

                    RICHARD
          All hands ondeck! Candace!
          You okay!?

Candace is strung out, still safely tethered to her lifeline. Without it, she would have been washed overboard. Water is everywhere. It's hard to tell which way is up or down.

                    RICHARD (CONT'D)
          Drop the main! Now!

                    CHAD
          I can't. The halyard is jammed!

                    CANDACE
          We're going to lose the mast!

The wind and noise are deafening. Candace's face shows sheer panic and fear. Daniel comes up on deck as another wave of icy seawater washes over everyone. The deck is awash with water and tangled ropes.

                    RICHARD
          We can't drop the main!

Forced to deal with their survival, Daniel has no second thoughts.

DANIEL

Get me up there! I'll cut the halyard
if I have ta!

He re-ties his sou'wester tighter under his chin and grabs the
bosun's harness. Richard shares a look of grave concern with
Daniel, then turns and starts barking out orders.

RICHARD

Chad, get the sea anchor off the bow!
Candace, take the helm!

Richard helps Daniel tie into a line. This storm is not letting up.
Candace tries to help her father untangle a line for Daniel.

RICHARD (CONT'D)

I can do this! Get back to the helm.
Keep her pointed into irons!

Daniel gives Candace a reassuring nod.

This is not the time for hurt feelings or crushed egos. Their lives
are at stake. Daniel climbs the mast up past the boom, then slowly
begins his ascent up the mast. The wind tears at the flapping
canvas sails.

Just past the spreaders, another huge wave breaks, tearing Daniel
away from the mast and throwing him hard into the main-
stay shroud.

Grimacing pain registers on Daniels face. He reaches for his back.
When he pulls his hand away, it's covered in blood.

DANIEL

Keep going! Higher!

He points towards the top of the mast. Richard frantically cranks the line through the winch.

At the top of the mast, Daniel hangs on with one arm, his mariner's knife gripped in his teeth. It's the last place on earth anyone would want to be. The halyard looks hopelessly jammed to one side of its sheave. Daniel works frantically, trying to pry the rope back up into its proper place. The tension eases off the main halyard between gusts, just long enough for Daniel to free the line. He waves frantically and yells. His voice is swallowed by the wind.

Chad responds by taking a wrap off his winch. The main sheet slowly starts to ease out through his hands.

At the top of the mast, the mainsail drops away. Daniel is left 55 feet above the deck with nothing but the roaring sea below him.

Richard eases up on the winch as Daniel starts his slow descent. He is completely spent. The driving rain washes his blood across the mainsail. Things are back in control.

INT. GALLEY - NIGHT

From the smash-up in the first knockdown, Dean has broken his collarbone. Richard is tending to it best he can. Candace lifts away layers of Daniel's wet, bloody clothing so she can take a better look at his injury. His back is badly bruised and deeply cut.

DANIEL

It's nothin'. Don't worry 'bout me.

CANDACE

Good thing is, I don't think you've
broken any ribs. But you are going to
need stiches.

RICHARD

That was a hell of a thing you did up
there, Daniel. You saved our lives.

DANIEL

And mine!

Wincing under Candace's care, Daniel cracks a radiant smile.

CANDACE

What are you grinning at? Are you
going into shock or something?

DANIEL

No, I was thinking about how much I
love this! I'm so pumped right now, I
can't even think straight.

RICHARD

(half joking)
Sailing isn't always this much fun.

DANIEL

No, it's the other way 'round. I've just
decided I'm going to finish my boat
and sail her 'round the world. I can't
think of anything I'd rather do. You
know what I'm saying?

                    RICHARD
        (amused)
        We'll get you properly fixed up when
        we get to Boston. I should get back
        topside. So much for night watches.
        With any luck, we might still have
        a race.

Richard heads up. Daniel looks at Dean.

                    DANIEL
        How you doing? You going to
        be okay?

Dean is in a lot of pain. Every movement of the boat causes him to
work at balancing, creating more pain.

                    DEAN
        I'll be fine. Just hand me that bottle
        before you go.

                    DANIEL
        Are you old enough to be drinking?

                    DEAN
        Give me the bottle!

EXT. BOSTON COAST – EARLY DAWN

The storm is subsiding. Through his binoculars, Chad spots one of
the other boats on the horizon.

Against Boston's cityscape, the flotilla of committee boats and the
finish line are in sight. Fifty-some hours of racing later, it all comes

down to the last few minutes. Richard's yacht crosses the finish line 12 minutes before the next competitor!

Yachts with their escort boats enter the marina, where banners fly and people wave. James stands on the dock waiting. Ropes are tossed and tied off. Richard steps onto the dock. He sees his wife and gives her a big hug.

Daniel and Chad help poor drunken Dean off the boat. James stands with Candace. They look about as compatible as Prince Charles and Lady Di. Medics arrive with a stretcher. Candace leaves James' side to help.

INT. THE STEWARTS' BOSTON HOME - DAY

Richard, still unshaven, wears his Boston Yacht Club blazer. The rest of the crew are all cleaned up. Chad looks weathered. Dean has his arm in a sling supporting his broken collarbone. Daniel, in his Lunenburg finery: a mended plaid shirt with badly worn corduroy pants proudly shares this moment with the others. Neither Richard nor Dean nor Chad seem the least bit concerned. Only when James and Candace make their entrance do the dynamics shift.

JAMES

If it isn't Braveheart draped in his --

Candace elbows James in the gut. James is caught off guard by her swift reaction.

JAMES (CONT'D)

-- my god look at him.

INT. BOSTON YACHT CLUB - EVENING

As Richard's crew arrives, Daniel is the toast of the evening.

> CANDACE
> Is that sailing around the world idea
> still working for you?

> RICHARD
> Or have you come back to
> your senses?

> DANIEL
> The truth be known, I'm hopelessly
> addicted. It's what I've got to do.

> JAMES
> We should get going, Candace. We'll
> catch up with you gentlemen later.
> Mrs. Stewart.

Candace looks back at her proud crew. She'd rather stay with them.

> RICHARD
> Have a good evening. We'll catch up
> to you later.

EXT. RICHARD'S YACHT - NIGHT

Safely moored inside the yacht club's marina. The winning crew is sharing a drink out of the Halifax/Boston Cup as they drink into the night.

> RICHARD
> I would just like to say, we had one
> hell of a season, and you gentlemen

are the best crew I have ever had the
privilege of sailing with. That was one
hell of a last race, you all should be
very proud.

>   CHAD
> I'd like to drink a toast. May the
> winds be steady and the seas calm,
> and God pray you have someone to
> climb your mast the day you're in
> a knockdown!

Everyone cheers. Chad gives a nod and a wink to Dean.

>   DEAN
> Daniel, we have something we'd like
> to present to you --

Chad pulls a sweater out from under one of the stowaways.

>   CHAD
> -- As a token of our thanks for saving
> our hides! I will never forget that
> storm as long as I live.

Daniel staggers to his feet and opens the sweater. On it is stitched
the Boston Yacht Club's crest.

>   DANIEL
> You guys are great, the best! This has
> been such an incredible summer. I
> don't know what to say.
> (suddenly remembers something)

Wait a minute! I almost forgot. No
one move!

Tipsy, he stumbles down into the galley. The laughter and celebrat-
ing continues. Finally, Daniel, sporting his new sweater and his
well-worn sou'wester, reappears on deck. From under his sweater
he pulls out his gifts. Sou'westers! He plunks one on each of
their heads.

>   DANIEL (CONT'D)
>   A little something in the way of
>   my thanks.

Each man laughs in turn as he receives his gift.

>   DANIEL (CONT'D)
>   I got one more down below for
>   Candace in case I don't see her before
>   I head back.

>   DEAN
>   I remember the first time I saw you
>   wearing one of these. I thought it was
>   the dumbest-looking thing. Now?
>   Thank you very much, Daniel.

Chad is drunk. His overeducated literary side takes over.

>   CHAD
>   What Dean is trying to say is that
>   he wishes he had -- had the insight
>   into the hat's true function and grace
>   before he went and condemned it as
>   being dumb. Daniel, I toast you and

accept your gift with all its intended
gestures. Thank you.

                    RICHARD
In other word's Chad, you're drunk!
Thank you, Daniel, this means a lot.
Just no more mast climbing when we
need you on deck!

EXT. RICHARD'S YACHT - NIGHT

It's late. The drinking is finally winding down. Dean is passed out.

                    CHAD
Dean, wake up! Let's get going.
That's right. Wave goodnight with
your broken wing. Daniel, we'll see
you next summer. It's been great.

                    DEAN
Goodnight, everyone.

Chad and Dean stagger down the dock.

Daniel lies passed out. Richard is still wearing his sou'wester as
he sips his rum. His contemplative eyes follow the rigging up to
the stars.

EXT. RICHARD'S YACHT - MORNING

Candace stands smiling into the cockpit. She's holding a thermos
and a couple of cups. Richard and Daniel lay passed out together.

CANDACE

Good morning! What time did you
guys finally pass out?

Richard's stirs, his sou'wester is down over his eyes.

RICHARD

It's morning? What time is it?

CANDACE

Eight-thirty. Daddy, you promised
you would take me out today.
I head back to school tomorrow!

She pours him some coffee.

CANDACE (CONT'D)

Is he alright?

She nods at Daniel, who is still passed out. He hasn't moved.

RICHARD

He'll live. I don't think he drinks
much. So, where do you want to go?
And are we alone, or we waiting for
your fiancé to join us?

CANDACE

James is hopefully still licking his
wounds as he tries to dry out. I'll go
below and make some breakfast. You
get us out of here and surprise me.

Richard sits up and pulls off his hat.

RICHARD

Hold on there, young lady. James
is where?

CANDACE

Gone! I broke it off with him
last night.

RICHARD

You're making this up, right?

CANDACE

It was great! You would have been so
proud of me. James had me so riled
up from the moment I got off the
boat till the moment I pushed him
off the dock.

RICHARD

Wait! You didn't really push him into
the harbour?

CANDACE

Oh, yes, I did! With all his stuffy
friends there to witness. I have never
felt so good. Today I am officially a
single woman.

RICHARD

Well I'm proud of you! For standing
up for yourself. Congratulations!

Candace heads below. Richard gives Daniel a shove.

                    RICHARD (CONT'D)
          Come on, kid. We're going
          sailing. Wakeup!

Daniel stirs.

                    DANIEL
          What day is it?

He sits up too fast, winces, squinting, his head aching and still not
actually awake.

                    DANIEL (CONT'D)
          I feel like my head is going to bust! I
          think I'm still drunk!

                    RICHARD
          Come on, it's only Monday. You've
          got all day to sober up.

                    DANIEL
          Ya but my bus ride, is going to take
          at least a day. I should have left
          last night.

                    RICHARD
          Relax! You can catch a ride with
          Swain in the morning. He's flying
          up first thing tomorrow to close up
          his place. You'll be there in plenty of
          time to get to work.

                    DANIEL
          Fly? Tomorrow? In the air? Flying?

RICHARD

Sure. You get home, dump your bag,
go to work.

He turns to get his coffee. Daniel pulls off his sweater and shirt,
then dives off the boat. He surfaces and flaps his arms like wings.

DANIEL

Yahoo! I've never been in a plane!

INT. GALLEY - DAY

Post-race, the place is in ruins. Candace, tries to clear a space to
work. Soggy gear hangs drying, the first-aid kit is strewn everywhere, the nav table is a mess of maps and empty bottles from the
night before. Daniel enters, soaking wet.

DANIEL

Excuse me, sorry I -- I just need
something dry to change into.

Candace looks at Daniel, shivering, dipping water everywhere.

CANDACE

What's with you and water? Don't
worry. I'll keep my back turned.

She turns and continues clearing and cleaning. She goes to lift a
pot that is stuck to another pot with stuff cooked on its sides. Wet
storm gear drips as Candace talks to the cupboards.

>   CANDACE (CONT'D)
>   I know the weather was rough, but
>   no one said anything about destroy-
>   ing the place.

Daniel shivers. He's not quite sure what to do. He has to get out of his wet clothes. There's nowhere to hide in such a small space. Finally, he pulls off his shirt.

Candace reaches for a cupboard. It has a mirror on the inside of the door. She uses it to watch Daniel get undressed as she continues her one-sided conversation.

>   CANDACE (CONT'D)
>   How much did you guys drink
>   last night?

Daniel towels off, sniffs a shirt, throws it away, and grabs another.

>   CANDACE (CONT'D)
>   After this year, I plan to spend more
>   time up in Lunenburg. Maybe I'll be
>   there when you finish your boat.

Daniel has his clean pants and shirt all lined up. The next thing to do is get out of his wet pants.

>   CANDACE (CONT'D)
>   Maybe I could rent part of your shed
>   for a studio.

>   DANIEL
>   Yeah, maybe.

                         CANDACE
              I made some coffee. It's up on deck.

Daniel drops his pants. He's not wearing any underwear. His back
is bandaged. The floor is slippery. He reaches for a towel.

                      CANDACE (CONT'D)
                 What do you feel like --
                 for breakfast?

Daniel, his back turned to Candace, remains very occupied, unaware
that she has turned to check him out more thoroughly than the
mirror permitted. Daniel carefully pulls on his shirt, easing it over
the bandage.

                          DANIEL
                 Sorry about the mess. We sure didn't
                 have much time for keeping things
                 neat the last couple days.

EXT. RICHARD'S YACHT - MORNING

The yacht is almost at the breakwater of the yacht club. The swells
are turning into small chop. The bow hits the first wave.

INT. GALLEY - MORNING

Daniel hops on one foot, struggling with his pants. Suddenly, he
slips on the wet floor. He lands on his butt, squirming in a panic to
get covered up.

                         CANDACE
                 Are you okay?

                    DANIEL
          No problem. I'll get down here
          and help straighten up once we
          get underway.

Daniel fights his way back up from a kneeling position as he reaches for his sweater. Caught off guard, Candace turns quickly, bumping her head on the open cupboard door.

                 DANIEL (CONT'D)
          You okay?

Slightly embarrassed, Candace slams the door as she reaches for a frying pan.

                   CANDACE
          Yeah, stupid cupboards never stay
          closed. Do you feel like some eggs?

Daniel comes around to make sure she didn't hurt herself.

                    DANIEL
          We missed you last night. Did you
          have a good time?

Candace holds back, still unsure of his feelings.

                   CANDACE
          Wish I could have partied a little
          harder with you guys. But I had a
          good night just the same.

EXT. RICHARD'S YACHT - DAY

Daniel returns to the cockpit from the bow.

> RICHARD
>
> How's your back?

> DANIEL
>
> Still a little tender. I suppose getting
> the stitches wet didn't help.

> RICHARD
>
> Candace! Could you throw me up
> the first-aid kit?

> CANDACE (O.S.)
>
> Who's hurt now?

> RICHARD
>
> Nobody. We're just changing
> Daniel's bandage.

EXT. RICHARD'S YACHT – MINUTES LATER

All three are back in the cockpit. Candace serves up breakfast. She
spots Richard's sou'wester hanging off the transom to the galley.
She grabs it and pulls it on, half to be funny and half to keep her
hair from blowing around.

> CANDACE
>
> Who's turning into the fisher-
> man, b'geez?

Richard reacts protectively towards his prize.

RICHARD

Hey, that's mine. You got your own.
Daniel gave each of us one last night.

Candace gives Daniel a curious look.

CANDACE

You have one for me?

DANIEL

Yes! I've got it with my stuff
down below.

CANDACE

Really? You got one for me?

DANIEL

Let me go get it.

He runs below and then returns a moment later.

DANIEL (CONT'D)

They're from home. Made by the
women there. By the looks of the
tartan inside, this one comes from
Peggy's Cove.

Candace takes her dad's off and gives it back. Daniel carefully shapes her hat and puts it on her head.

CANDACE

This is so wonderful!

RICHARD

This is one of those things that, if I
had bought it for myself, it would
have just been a souvenir.

CANDACE

This makes it so special. How do I
look? Thank you, Daniel.

Candace leans forward to kiss Daniel on his cheek and give him
a hug.

INT. THE STEWARTS' BOSTON HOME, BEDROOM - NIGHT

It's late, and the house is dark. Daniel is packing. There's a knock at
the door. Daniel opens it, and Candace slips in.

CANDACE

I wanted to give you this before you
had everything packed.

She hands Daniel a rolled-up paper tied with a ribbon. Daniel
unrolls it. It's one of her drawings from their summer.

DANIEL

Look here. That's me and me boat.

CANDACE

I had the best summer ever, and I
wanted to thank you for it.

DANIEL

So did I.

                    CANDACE
          You have to let me know how
          things are going with your work
          and the boat, stuff like that. I'll be
          writing you.

                    DANIEL
          Thanks for all the sailing lessons and
          the help with my boat and stuff.

Candace steps forward.

                    CANDACE
          The pleasure was all mine.

They hug like friends, only the hug lasts a little too long. They pull
back and look into each other's eyes. Candace's lips meet Daniel's.
Daniel wraps his arms around her, one hand resting in the small of
her back. Candace's hands slowly untuck Daniel's shirt. Her warm
hands touch his back. Daniel winces.

                    CANDACE (CONT'D)
          Sorry.

She reaches out and flicks the light switch. The room goes dark.
Moonlight fills the room with a soft blue glow.

                    DANIEL
          You sure this is such a good idea?

                    CANDACE
          Shhhh --

They continue to kiss, embraced in a slow dance. Daniel starts to pull on Candace's blouse at her waist.

> DANIEL
>
> Should we be doing this?

> CANDACE
>
> Shhhh --

Daniel caresses Candace's stomach with his thumbs and then his open hands slide to her naked waist. Candace takes a deep breath, like a gasp. Daniel continues to caress her waist then up her back. Candace pushes in closer and pulls Daniel's T-shirt up over his head. She kisses his chest, his neck. Daniel's hands tremble as if raw electricity is flowing through him. His T-shirt off, Candace kisses him with unleashed passion. This is it! He picks Candace up in his strong arms and lays her on his bed. The steel sprung bed frame lets out a loud squeak, shattering their focus.

> CANDACE (CONT'D)
>
> Oh great!

They giggle. Daniel puts a finger up to his lips.

> DANIEL
>
> Shhhh --

> CANDACE
>
> This bed is too noisy. Someone's going to hear us.

> DANIEL
>
> What do we do?

                    CANDACE
        Honestly, I only came in here to
        say goodnight.

                    DANIEL
        You picked a great way to say it.

They try to kiss quietly and caress each other, but the bed is not cooperating. Finally, Candace stands.

                    CANDACE
        Well, you'll just have to wait for me
        then. Won't you?

                    DANIEL
        I'll have to think about this. Will
        I wait? I think we should at least
        discuss this a little further.

Daniel slides onto the floor, pulling the covers with him. She shakes her head.

                    CANDACE
        You're being very resourceful
        this evening.

Candace kneels down as Daniel unbuttons her blouse. She pulls a few remaining pins from her hair.

They make love in the moonlight.

INT. BEDROOM - NIGHT

It's late as Candace tiptoes to the door. Daniel is fast asleep.

CANDACE

Sweet dreams, Mr. Tanner.

INT. THE STEWARTS' BOSTON HOME, FOYER — EARLY MORNING

Daniel rushes around getting ready to leave as Richard and his wife look on.

DANIEL

Thank you again for everything. Be
sure to say goodbye to Candace and
Dean for me.

RICHARD

She must still be sleeping. Candace!
Come say goodbye to Daniel.

Candace comes out of her room all sleepy, dressed in pajamas and her bathrobe.

CANDACE

Bye, Daniel. Have a good winter.
Get that boat done. We'll see you
next summer.

DANIEL

I'll write. Bye, everyone. See you
all next summer. Thanks again
for everything!

With that, he's out the door and down the steps into Swain's waiting car.

EXT. THE STEWARTS' BOSTON HOME - MORNING

Dean Eilertson

Daniel looks back and sees Candace waving from an upstairs balcony.

INT. TANNER BOAT SHED - DAY

Candace's drawing hangs nicely over the workbench, obscured momentarily by a cloud of cold breath. Daniel is all bundled up. It's freezing. He loads wood into the stove. He picks up his coffee cup and turns it upside down. A frozen chunk of coffee falls to the floor. The letter from Candace is Daniel's only comfort.

> CANDACE (V.O.)
> Dear Daniel, your last letter sounded
> like you were making good progress
> on the boat. I was talking to Chad
> the other day. Are you sitting? He
> told me about this guy at the club
> here who has decided to totally refit
> his boat with all new hardware! I
> asked Father to check into it for
> you. The old stuff is still apparently
> in great shape. It's just not "state of
> the art." Keep your fingers crossed.
> I'll keep you posted. School this year
> is taking forever. I keep looking at
> my calendar and wishing for spring
> to hurry up. I wore the hat you
> gave me in the rain the other day. I
> will admit to getting the odd stare.
> Hope all is well with you. I miss you.
> XO Candace

As Daniel finishes the letter, he looks concerned.

INT. BOSTON COLLEGE, STUDIO SPACE - DAY

Candace reads her letter from Daniel. Around her are an assortment of drawings of Daniel's boat, his shed, Lunenburg, and one of the original Roué drawings. On her sculpture stand, Candace is trying to work on a bust of Daniel from memory.

> DANIEL (V.O.)
> Dear Candace, I've made a promise
> to myself today not to spend another
> winter here. It's minus twenty. On
> top of that, we just finished getting
> another huge dump of snow! It's
> taking forever to get things ready for
> paint. I feel like I've been sanding
> and scraping for months. But the
> worst is definitely over. Work at the
> yards has wound down for winter.
> In other words, everything is frozen
> solid! Which allows me to spend
> most of my time here in my little
> shed working on my boat. I sure
> miss the sailing (and you). Thanks
> again for that book on navigating.
> I've already got the first leg of my
> trip planned! When is spring coming
> again? Daniel

INT. LEGION - NIGHT

Daniel and John are talking and having a beer.

> JOHN GREEK
> That'll save you a ton of money, boy.

DANIEL

That's not the point, John. I can't take
charity like that. I don't want to end
up indebted to anyone, especially
the Stewarts.

JOHN GREEK

Why do you call it charity? I see it as
friends helping out. If I had rigging,
I'd give it to you too.

DANIEL

This is a whole lot different. With
them I can't return the favour.
Nothing I can give them will ever be
good enough.

JOHN GREEK

I think you're reading way too much
into this, Daniel. He sees you have
a goal, and as a friend, Rich is just
trying to help you with it, is all.

DANIEL

That'd be fine if his daughter wasn't
someone I was trying to impress.
What's she going to think of me if
all I can do is take handouts from her
old man and folks like that?

JOHN GREEK

You'll have to ask Candace that one.

                    DANIEL
No. I've decided. I'll take their help,
but I won't complicate things by
getting involved.

                  JOHN GREEK
Good luck on that one. Someday
you're going to learn that letting
people help isn't so bad.

INT. TANNER BOAT SHED - day

Daniel pries open a wooden crate, revealing winches, pulleys, cleats,
and so on.

                  DANIEL (V.O.)
Dear Candace, the crate arrived
today. There's enough here for two
boats! One more coat of varnish
on the bright work, and the first
thing I'll start installing will be the
winches. I've enclosed a cheque to
cover your dad's shipping and crating
costs. Please thank him for me. I just
gave the sail loft here my deposit,
so they can get started on my sails.
That should be the last big hurdle.
The galley is shaping up. The foundry
here had an old cast-iron coal heater
stove that they let me have for next
to nothing! So, things are coming
along fine. I can't wait for spring to
arrive, so I can finally open those two

big doors and send this girl down the
ramp into the water.

Candace sets the letter down and walks over to a window overlooking the city. Daniel hasn't mentioned a word about their relationship.

EXT. LUNENBURG HARBOUR – DAY

It's spring. Snow melts, and icicles drip. There's still ice on the shores.

INT. TANNER BOAT SHED – DAY

The double doors swing open. Daniel and John walk down the ramp to the water's edge and then turn to look back into the shed. The boat is finished. It has a pale-yellow hull and forest-green trim, just like the Tanner dory.

> JOHN GREEK
> That's three generations of Tanners
> thar, boy. You must be proud.

> DANIEL
> Do you like the colours?

> JOHN GREEK
> That's a fine touch. You've done great
> by her, son. Your old man would be
> so damn proud of you.

                    DANIEL
          I called you here today to ask if you'd
          help me get her in the water.

                  JOHN GREEK
          Have you got a name for her yet?

                    DANIEL
          The same name she was always going
          to have, Dreammaker. I'm hoping
          I can get Candace to paint it on
          for me.

                  JOHN GREEK
          That's as damn fine a name as I ever
          heard. I'd be honoured to give ya a
          hand. Here you'll be needing this.

John pulls a bottle of champagne out from under his coat and
hands it to Daniel. John smiles and slaps him on the back.

              JOHN GREEK (CONT'D)
          Go on boy! You smack her with
          this. I'll knock the blocks out from
          under her.

INT. TANNER BOAT SHED - DAY

A sledgehammer sets the wedges. The supports fall away. In
SLOW MOTION, the bottle swings in and smashes over the bow.
Dreammaker starts on her slide towards the sea, ending with her
bow as it hits the water, disappearing in a cloud of spray.

EXT. LUNENBURG HARBOUR - DAY

Dean Eilertson

Daniel pilots Dreammaker as Josef tows him into the NSP repair yard behind his lobster boat. A crowd of workers stand watching their arrival. The only thing left to do is step her mast.

> JOSEF SORENSEN
> What the hell are ya dragging in
> here? Hey boys, just don't stand thar
> gawkin'! Get some line, an' give him
> a hand! Some men do the strangest
> things with their time off.

EXT. NSP REPAIR YARD DOCKS - DAY

Daniel talks with Josef, his foreman.

> DANIEL
> What do ya think?

> JOSEF SORENSEN
> She's a beaut. I haven't seen somethin'
> that's needed sails for years. Almost
> forgot what they look like.

> DANIEL
> So, it's alright to moor her here for
> a bit? I was hoping to use the cherry
> picker to step the mast.

> JOSEF SORENSEN
> I don't see no problem thar. No,
> that'd be fine. What da hell you plan
> to do with her?

DANIEL

Sail her around the world! That's
what she's built for.

JOSEF SORENSEN

I always saw ya as a bit of a
dreamer. What're you naming her,
HMS Tanner?

DANIEL

Dreammaker.

JOSEF SORENSEN

Dreammaker? For the dreamer.
Kinda fits, don't it, boy? Well, we'll
get that mast up thar for ya alright.
I see ya got some nice fittin's on har
too! Nice job, real nice!

EXT. TANNER BOAT SHED - DAY

A car slows to a stop at the top of the road and then pulls in.

It's Dean and Candace. Candace jumps out and runs towards the
shed door. She knocks, hoping to surprise Daniel. She's carrying a
book on Pacific Rim sailing adventures.

DEAN

Are you sure this is such a good idea?
I don't know of anyone who enjoys
being surprised.

                          CANDACE
            He doesn't have a phone! I'm dying
            to see the boat!

INT. TANNER BOAT SHED - DAY

The door swings open, Candace's pace slows to a stop, as she sets
the book on the table. The shed is strikingly empty. Dean heads
over to open the big double doors. No boat in the bay.

                          CANDACE
                 Do you think he's gone?

Gloria enters carrying a bag of groceries. She's immediately
protective.

                          GLORIA
                 Can I help you?

Candace's and Gloria's eyes meet.

                           DEAN
                 We're looking for Daniel. We were
                 hoping to say hello and take a look at
                 his boat.

                          GLORIA
                 Daniel's at work. He won't be home
                 till later.

                          CANDACE
                 Home?

Gloria and Candace are not hitting it off.

GLORIA

Yeah. He usually doesn't finish work
till 4:30. I never see him much earlier
than that.

Candace is shaken. She barely looks at Dean before she exits.

CANDACE

I'll wait in the car. Excuse me.

Dean tries to follow as quickly as possible.

DEAN

Sorry to barge in. We should have
waited till we knew he was home.
Could you tell Daniel we were here?

GLORIA

No problem. Does your friend need
some water? She looked a bit faint.

DEAN

She'll be fine. Thanks.

Gloria grins as she watches Dean leave, very aware of what has
just transpired.

INT. DEAN'S CAR - DAY

Tears stream down Candace's face as she stares out her side window.
Dean nervously keeps checking over at her as he drives.

                           DEAN

Candace, maybe it's not what you
think. It's not like you're in love with
the guy. I mean, what's going on
here? Come on, sis. It's not the end
of the world or anything.

Candace sobs even loader.

                      DEAN (CONT'D)

Or is it?

                         CANDACE

Just stay out of it!

                           DEAN

Oh boy! I'll go talk to him tomorrow.

                         CANDACE

I don't want your help. I should have
known it wouldn't last.

                           DEAN

You are in love with him then?!
What about sailing and stuff like
that? You're sure to run into each
other sooner or later.

                         CANDACE

I'll get over it. Two can play
this game.

INT. TANNER BOAT SHED – EARLY DUSK

Daniel enters and sees the bag of groceries on his table. Gloria is waiting up in the loft, lying naked in Daniel's bed.

> GLORIA
>
> I thought you might need a few
> things. Why don't you come up here
> and say thank you?

Daniel reacts.

> DANIEL
>
> Gloria? What are you doing?

> GLORIA
>
> Hello, Gloria. How are you, Gloria?
> Thank you for the kind gesture,
> Gloria. We are neighbours, ya know!

> DANIEL
>
> Do I look like I need any kind
> gestures? I know I sure as hell didn't
> ask for the likes of you to come make
> herself welcome in my bed.

Gloria is angry and hurt. She gets up from Daniel's bed, pulls her dress back on over her head, and starts her slow descent down the stairs. Daniel picks up the bag of groceries, so he can give them back. He spots the book.

> DANIEL (CONT'D)
>
> Where did this book come from?

GLORIA

It's from that rich bitch little friend
of yours! May be coming here to have
her way for another summer?

DANIEL

You're one to talk. Now take this stuff
and get out of here! And mind your
own damn business.

Gloria grabs her coat and her bag of groceries.

GLORIA

Last chance, Daniel. I only offer
once, and there's still so many lonely
cold nights ahead. We could have so
much fun.

DANIEL

Go on! Get the hell out of my
place and mind your own sorrow-
ful business!

GLORIA

Well, well, mister high and mighty.
Why don't you just go an' fuck
yourself then.

She exits, slamming the door so hard it almost comes off its hinges.
Daniel looks down at the book. Frustrated, he slams it on the table.

DANIEL

Thanks for droppin' by! Shit!!

INT. FLYING BRIDGE BAR - NIGHT

Some people play pool while others dance. It's far from busy. A bunch of guys Daniel recognizes from the yacht club come up the stairs. The last two are Dean and Candace. Daniel gets up from the bar.

> DANIEL
> Candace, Dean! Hey!

Dean joins his friends. Hearing her name, Candace moves coldly towards Daniel.

> CANDACE
> Save me a chair. I'll be right there.

Daniel approaches with his arms out to meet her.

> DANIEL
> How ya doin'? When did you
> get here?

> CANDACE
> This afternoon.

> DANIEL
> Is your dad up too?

> CANDACE
> No. Just Dean and me.

Candace hauls off and slaps Daniel across the face. Tears of hurt and anger begin to flow.

CANDACE (CONT'D)
You son of a bitch! How could you?

DANIEL
Woe–woe calm down! - it's not what
you think --

CANDACE
No. It's what I saw!

DANIEL
Look, I don't even like Gloria.

CANDACE
What's that supposed to mean? You
only screw around with people you
don't like?

Tears running down her face, Candace is too upset to talk anymore.
She runs out. Daniel turns to Dean.

DANIEL
I can explain every --

DEAN
Explain to someone else. You've obvi-
ously already done enough damage!
Here I thought we were friends?
Now get lost, asshole.

DANIEL
Woe! Down boy. I don't mind you
givin' me shit. Just don't you start
calling me names.

                              DEAN
           You brought this one on yourself,
           smart boy.

                             DANIEL
           Look, Dean, let's cut with the insults.
           I'm trying to talk to ya.

                              DEAN
           I think you've already said enough.

Dean takes a swing at Daniel. Daniel takes the hit but doesn't
attempt to hit back. He stops Dean's next swing.

                             DANIEL
           Dean!

Dean pushes Daniel's arm away and then readies himself to fight.
Dean's friends stand by, ready to help.

                              DEAN
           Come on! Asshole!

Daniel looks at his good friend in disbelief. He shakes his head as
he throws some money down on the bar and exits down the stairs.

INT. TANNER BOAT SHED – EARLY MORNING

Daniel mopes around. He looks like shit. He pours himself some
coffee, picks up Candace's gift, and heads to the double doors.
He opens them and slumps to the floor. He takes in his changing
world. The book lies on the floor near him. He picks it up. On the
inside cover, Candace has written a note.

CANDACE (V.O.)
To Captain D. Tanner, I am so
proud of you, my maker of boats and
dreams. May the gentle winds of life
take you wherever you want to go.
XO Candace

Tears start well up in his eyes. An emotion just discovered. One
that he cannot control. He sobs, hugging his knees to his chest,
rocking himself. Nobody is there to hear him or comfort him. He
is utterly alone.

EXT. TANNER BOAT SHED - DAY

Dreammaker is finished and anchored out in front of Daniel's shed.
The June bugs can be heard in the trees, it's well into early summer.
The yachts of the rich are back, out racing on the water.

INT. TANNER BOAT SHED - DAY

Daniel is up in the loft lying on his bed, staring up at the ceiling.
The two big doors are open.

JOHN GREEK (O.S.)
Day like this, I'd be out there sailing,
not lying around moppin'.

Daniel sits up and peers over the edge of the loft.

DANIEL
Hey, John.

JOHN GREEK

I haven't seen you for a while. What
you been doing with yourself?

DANIEL

Work mostly. Gettin' everyone back
in the water for lobster season.

John points to Daniel's boat anchored out in the cove.

JOHN GREEK

Have you at least had her sails
up yet?

DANIEL

I sailed her back here.

JOHN GREEK

So, when did you plan on inviting
me out? Matter of fact, I'm a touch
pissed you haven't called.

That's all Daniel needs, someone else angry or disappointed
with him.

DANIEL

You got time today?

JOHN GREEK

Let me grab my stuff before you
change your mind.

EXT. COVE - DAY

It's a breezy day. They row the dory out to Dreammaker. John hanks the jib to the forestay. Daniel hoists his crisp new mainsail up the mast. John takes up the slack through a winch. Both sails fill. Daniel's spirits lift. Despite the situation with Candace, he's proud of his accomplishment.

> DANIEL
> Here we go. What do you think?

> JOHN GREEK
> She's beautiful! How does she feel?

> DANIEL
> Hell, she steers herself. Here, you
> take her out.

Daniel proudly hands John the tiller. He goes forward to make some final adjustments. As he returns from the bow, he stops to check the mast.

> DANIEL (CONT'D)
> Feels good, doesn't it?

> JOHN GREEK
> Wish I had a camera. You'd make a
> good picture.

They're heading out of the bay, out past the yacht club. Daniel's expression changes. Richard's yacht is moored with Richard, Dean, and Candace out working on it.

> DANIEL
> I'll get the stove going. You want
> some coffee, John?

JOHN GREEK

Hey, don't leave me up here alone,
boy. That's all I need ta do is run yer'
boat aground!

DANIEL

Just keep her in the middle all the
way out. I'll be a couple minutes. Yell
if you need me.

Daniel disappears below. From the shore, Richard spots the boat
and waves. John gives a friendly wave back. The others turn to see
who Richard is waving at. It's the first time any of them have seen
the boat finished.

EXT. RICHARD'S YACHT – DAY

Richard points at Dreammaker.

RICHARD

Will you look at that! Goddamn,
now that is one beautiful boat.

CHAD

Who's that at the helm?

RICHARD

Looks like John Greek. They must be
taking her out for a shakedown.

CHAD

Daniel sure did an amazing job.

                    RICHARD
          Yeah, doesn't seem like that long ago
          he was just talking about it. Candace,
          you've been in touch with him. What
          are his plans?

Candace looks at her father. No one has told him what happened
on her earlier spring visit.

                    CANDACE
          I don't know. Dean's the only one
          whose seen him lately.

Richard can't believe his ears.

                    RICHARD
          I thought you two were writing back
          and forth?

                    CANDACE
          We were for a while. I haven't heard
          from him in months.

                    RICHARD
          I thought --

                    CANDACE
          Is that box of rain gear still in
          the car?

                    RICHARD
          Yeah, in the trunk.

                          CANDACE
                Can I get the keys, please?

With that Candace heads off the boat. A confused Richard looks
to Dean.

EXT. DREAMMAKER – DAY

John is still at the tiller.

                          JOHN GREEK
                So, boy, when do you think you'll
                head her out?

                          DANIEL
                Right after the fair. I'm done here.

                          JOHN GREEK
                Oh, I see.

                          DANIEL
                Yeah. Once I get out of here, things
                should start to look up.

                          JOHN GREEK
                Want some advice?

                          DANIEL
                Do I have a choice?

                          JOHN GREEK
                Nope! You still got some troubles
                here you're not facing head on.
                No man has ever outrun himself.

You've still got things here that need
sortin' out.

Daniel doesn't say a word. John has just touched on the core of
his dilemma.

> JOHN GREEK (CONT'D)
> See, I think you've got feelings for
> that girl of Rich's. Not only that, I
> think you just might want her in your
> life. Only, me thinks you got no self-
> confidence to go get what's yours.

> DANIEL
> A rich girl like that doesn't need the
> likes of me.

> JOHN GREEK
> Have you even tried to ask her?

> DANIEL
> Haven't had the chance since she last
> stormed outta my place.

> JOHN GREEK
> Are you ever going to ask her?

> DANIEL
> I can't -- she thinks I got a girlfriend.

> JOHN GREEK
> How the hell you manage that?

DANIEL

She came by my place a couple
months back, while I was at work.
Gloria from down the way was there.
I guess she got the impression then.

JOHN GREEK

Did you ever explain?

DANIEL

Yeah. Tried that same night right to
her face. Now they're all pissed at me,
the whole damn family. I guess I hurt
a lot of feelings.

JOHN GREEK

Who are you hurting now? You've
got a say in your own destiny, ya
know. Right now, all you're being is a
lousy martyr, and doin' a hell of a job!

Daniel doesn't argue back. He knows John is right. If only he could
swallow his pride.

DANIEL

Want me to take over for a bit?

John sees Daniel is hurting. It's time to back off.

JOHN GREEK

Yeah. I've said my two bits worth.
Have you got your head hooked up? I
gotta piss something furious.

John heads down below deck, leaving Daniel in the cockpit.

> DANIEL
> There's a honey bucket down there
> somewhere, John.

Daniel looks at his compass and then back towards the yacht club. Which direction to take? He sighs.

> DANIEL (CONT'D)
> Who am I fooling?

INT. TANNER BOAT SHED - DAY

Daniel is busy organizing the supplies he'll be needing for his journey.

EXT. NSP REPAIR YARD — DAY

Daniel eats his lunch with Josef.

> JOSEF SORENSEN
> So, Daniel, when do ya plan on
> shipping outta here?

> DANIEL
> Right after I win that dory race.

Josef pulls out an old pipe and stuffs it with tobacco as Daniel continues to eat.

> JOSEF SORENSEN
> Then that's it? Gone?

DANIEL

Yeah, that's pretty much it. If I wait
much longer, I'll miss the winds I
need to get me south.

JOSEF SORENSEN

You don't need to tell me. I've sailed a
tad myself, ya know.

DANIEL

That's right, fishing the Grand Banks.

Josef lights his pipe.

JOSEF SORENSEN

No, that was later. This was back
when I was more your age. I was crew
on a hundred-foot merchant schooner called the Francis Drake.

DANIEL

That was my granddad's first ship!

JOSEF SORENSEN

That's right. The ol' bastard worked us
hard too, ya know. But still, it was the
best t'ing I ever did.

DANIEL

Where all did you go?

JOSEF SORENSEN

Oh – Singapore - Java, China, Tahiti.
That's where I got this --

He shows Daniel his faded Tahitian tribal tattoo.

> DANIEL
>
> Wow. How long were you gone?

> JOSEF SORENSEN
>
> Six years in all. Till we ran her
> aground on some reef just off
> Indonesia. We was laid up for repairs
> for almost four months. I'll never
> forget dis one drunken night, this
> chief offered me his pretty daughter's
> hand in marriage.

> DANIEL
>
> What happened?

> JOSEF SORENSEN
>
> Oh, I already had a girl back here
> waiting for me.

> DANIEL
>
> I can't believe you came back.
> Everything you're sayin' sounds way
> more exciting.

> JOSEF SORENSEN
>
> Yeah, but I'd given my word before I
> left that I'd come back for her.

He rubs his scruffy chin. He wouldn't have done it any other way.

> DANIEL
>
> So, you did? You came back?

> JOSEF SORENSEN
>
> What use was I to anyone if my word
> was no good? When we finally got
> back, I got all cleaned up an' shaved,
> put my final pay in my pocket --

(points to a dock not far away)

> I walked right off dat dock thar and
> straight up to her house. Top of Main
> Street. Lucky for me, she'd waited.

His pipe has gone out. He rummages around in the pockets of his bib coveralls.

> JOSEF SORENSEN (CONT'D)
>
> You got a match?

Daniel is still staring at the dock, caught up in Josef's story.

> DANIEL
>
> Pardon? Sorry, no, I quit.

INT. CHESTER YACHT CLUB - NIGHT

A party. The members celebrate their return for the summer. Some of Candace's friends from school have come up for a visit. Others are recognizable from past club events. One CLUB MEMBER approaches Richard.

> CLUB MEMBER
>
> What say, ol' chap? Are you going
> to dominate this year's series and

humiliate your fellow members as
badly as you did last summer?

RICHARD
If I can help it.

CLUB MEMBER
What secret weapon(s) this time
around? You put one cracker of a
crew together last summer. Say what!

The other members join in on the good-natured ribbing.

RICHARD
Allow me to make a toast.

They all raise their glasses.

RICHARD (CONT'D)
May I wish you all the best of luck,
for you will need it!

His words are followed by laughter and the clinking of glasses.

CLUB MEMBER #2
(a Scotsman)
Here's to us!

At another table, Candace is sitting with her cousin, DAVID, and
her friends from school, MARY-BETH, LOUISE, LEANNE, and JOANNE.

DAVID
This is quite the group. Where's this
guy you spent all winter pining for?

MARY-BETH

Yes, we're dying to meet this gentle,
kind hunk of an "alpha male."

CANDACE

He dumped me.

DAVID

When did this happen? Ah,
Candace! This guy, obviously doesn't
know what he's just lost.

LOUISE

Yes! Believe me, it's his loss,
not yours.

CANDACE

Right.

MARY-BETH

Lousy stinkin' men. They're all the
same. Well, aren't they?

LOUISE

You can trust them about as far as
you can throw them.

LEANNE

This will cheer you up. What's the
useless piece of skin at the end of a
man's you know what?

Talk about bad timing. Everyone thinks for a bit, and then they
give up.

LEANNE (CONT'D)

The man! Ha-ha! Get it?

DAVID

Enough with the male bashing. We're
not all assholes.

EXT. THE STEWARTS' HOUSE, BACKYARD - DAY

Candace's friends are all stretched out sunbathing. David is
giving Louise a massage. Candace is inside at the kitchen window
looking out.

JOANNE

Who's up for a swim? Come
on, everyone!

LOUISE

Thanks, David, I needed that. Are
you coming?

DAVID

Not just yet. I want to visit with
Candace for a bit. You go ahead.

Everyone heads towards the lake, playing catch, shouting, and
carrying on. Candace comes out from the house carrying a tray
of lemonade.

CANDACE

Hey, where are they going?

DAVID

For a swim.

CANDACE

Do you have enough energy left to
give another massage? I don't know
why, but my neck and shoulders are
seized right up.

DAVID

Come, darling. Lay down here and
surrender yourself to me.

Candace sets down the tray and lays out on the blanket. David
is muscular, tanned, and handsome. The fact that he plays for the
other team doesn't bother her in the least. They are cousins and the
best of friends. He starts by dripping oil on Candace's back.

DAVID (CONT'D)

God, you've got knots here the size of
golf balls. You might want to loosen
your shoulder straps, so I can get
right to work.

EXT. THE STEWARTS' HOUSE - DAY

Daniel is at the front door. MRS. STEWART opens the door.

MRS. STEWART

Hello, Daniel. My, we haven't seen
you for quite a while. How have
you been?

DANIEL

Working hard. The yard's been very
busy. Is Candace here?

MRS. STEWART

Yes, she is. She's got some friends up
here from school. They're out in the
backyard. Go through the kitchen.
You know the way.

DANIEL

Thanks. Nice talking to you.

MRS. STEWART

Tell them lunch will be in about
fifteen. You'll stay, won't you?

DANIEL

I don't know yet. Maybe.

Daniel walks through the kitchen towards the screen door. Candace
is lying face down, her arms stretched out above her head. David is
straddling her, his hands moving sensually up her bare back.

CANDACE

God, you're good at this. I'm so lucky
to have someone like you.

Daniel is dumbfounded. He can hardly believe his eyes or ears.
Neither one notices him looking out through the screen door. They
both break out laughing. He can't hear what they're laughing about,
but what he sees is enough. He turns to exit just as Mrs. Stewart
enters the kitchen.

MRS. STEWART

Did you find her?

DANIEL

Yes. Thanks, I'll be going now.

MRS. STEWART

You're not staying for lunch?
(starts to open the screen door)
Well, it was nice to see you again,
Daniel. Do drop by again. We
miss you.

Candace looks up.

CANDACE

Mum, who were you just talking to?

MRS. STEWART

Daniel. Didn't he come out here?

CANDACE

No. What did he want?

MRS. STEWART

That's funny. He just left.

Candace rolls over and looks at David.

CANDACE

Holy shit! He probably thought you
were my boyfriend or something.

DAVID

What are you saying?

                    CANDACE
          Don't you see? Now the tables have
          turned. He's getting a bit of his
          own medicine.

Candace's mind is going a million miles per minute.

                    DAVID
          Is this guy the jealous type? You and
          I could pretend to be serious, parade
          around town together.

                    CANDACE
          Daniel doesn't even have the right to
          be jealous.

                    DAVID
          I thought you wanted to get back
          with the guy! This is no way to start.

                    CANDACE
          I do, but on my own terms. This is
          harmless compared to what he did
          to me.

EXT. TANNER BOAT SHED - DAWN

At first light, John rows Daniel, out to Dreammaker in Daniel's dory.

                    JOHN GREEK
          You're sure you got everything?

                    DANIEL
          I can always pick stuff up as I go.

JOHN GREEK

I thought you were stickin' around for
the fair. How come you're in such an
all-fired hurry to leave now?

DANIEL

I'm worried about the weather.
Everything's ready. I don't want to
delay any more than I have to.

JOHN GREEK

It jus' seems like you're trying to
slip away in the night. No good-
byes, nothin'.

DANIEL

I'd get too weirded out. It's better
this way.

JOHN GREEK

Too bad you won't be at your own
going-away party.

DANIEL

What do ya mean?

JOHN GREEK

Bunch of us thought we'd give you a
send-off. You know, some of the fellas
from the yard. Rick mentioned he
and your ol' crew wanted in on it.

DANIEL

That's awful nice of all ya. Just tell
'em --

JOHN GREEK

Did ya ever sort things out with your
lady friend?

DANIEL

No need. She's got herself a handsome new fella. I think things are
workin' out well for her. I wish her all
the best.

JOHN GREEK

That's too bad. Least you're not
leaving here all unsettled or nothin'.

They pull up alongside Dreammaker. Daniel climbs aboard as John
starts to hand up the last of his things.

JOHN GREEK (CONT'D)

So, here we are.

DANIEL

Thanks again, John. For everything,
I mean.

They shake hands.

JOHN GREEK

You take care. Take her good and
easy, and don't push yourself. I'll be
praying for ya.

John pushes off and starts rowing back.

> JOHN GREEK (CONT'D)
> I hate long goodbyes. We'll see ya.
> Make sure you don't forget where
> you're from.

Daniel waves goodbye. The morning sun is just above the horizon.

EXT. DREAMMAKER - MORNING

Daniel is on deck drinking coffee and going over some charts. Dolphins appear and swim along with the boat.

EXT. LUNENBURG FAIR - MORNING

Crowds of people arrive for the festivities.

INT. RICHARD'S CAR - MORNING

Richard and Candace drive past Daniel's place on their way to the yacht club.

> CANDACE
> Daddy, could you stop for a second? I
> want to wish Daniel good luck with
> his race.

> RICHARD
> Why don't you ask him to join us for
> our race! We could sure use the help.

> CANDACE
> Let me just try to open the door
> from my side first.

EXT. TANNER'S BOAT SHED - MORNING

As she enters the yard, something isn't right. Everything is either tarped or put away. She gets to the door and finds the brass padlock on the hasp.

Candace comes back out of Daniel's driveway and gets into the car.

> CANDACE (CONT'D)
> I think he's gone?!

> RICHARD
> What do you mean gone?

> CANDACE
> I mean gone as in sailed. The
> whole place is locked up. There's no
> one there.

EXT. DREAMMAKER - MORNING

Daniel sits staring out to sea as the sun gently rises.

MEMORY FLASH

John rows Daniel out to his boat in the dory.

> JOHN GREEK
> That's too bad. Least you're not
> leaving here all unsettled or nothin'.

MEMORY FLASH

Laughing, Candace dumps a pail of water over Daniel's head with James looking on in the distance.

MEMORY FLASH

That first afternoon Candace showed up at the boat shed.

MEMORY FLASH

Candace proudly shows Daniel the sliver.

MEMORY FLASH

Candace tries on her new sou'wester.

EXT. DREAMMAKER - EVENING

The sun is setting. Daniel is still sitting there, thinking.

MEMORY FLASH

Daniel talks to John in the boat shed.

> DANIEL
> You come into the world with
> nothing, and you leave with the same.

> JOHN GREEK
> That's for when you're dead, son.
> Life's about living, falling in
> love, experiencing and sharin' it
> with others.

EXT. DREAMMAKER - DAY

Unshaven and looking more weathered, Daniel looks depressed.

MEMORY FLASH

Josef talks to Daniel in the repair yard.

>JOSEF SORENSEN
>What use was I to anyone if my word
>was no good?

MEMORY FLASH

Candace stands up from the bed at her parents' Boston home.

>CANDACE
>Well, you'll just have to wait for me.

>DANIEL
>I'll have to think about this. Will
>I wait? I think we should at least
>discuss this a little further.

She shakes her head as she laughs.

>CANDACE
>My you are being very resourceful
>this evening.

MEMORY FLASH

Pretending to be asleep, he watches as she tucks her blouse back in and does up her skirt. Her hair remains tousled.

Candace tiptoes to the door.

> CANDACE
> Sweet dreams, Mr. Tanner.

EXT. OFF THE MAINE COAST - DAY

Daniel pushes the tiller hard left and brings the boat into a jibe. He heads for land somewhere south of Portsmouth.

EXT. A QUIET MARINA IN MAINE - NIGHT

The air is calm. Dreammaker is anchored. A warm glow shines from her porthole windows.

INT. DREAMMAKER GALLEY - NIGHT

Daniel is working on the boat's engine. He's cleaning the fuel filter with a rag and solvent. As he turns to reach for a wrench, he accidently knocks over the pan of solvent. It seeps all over the galley floor.

With only a kerosene lantern for light, Daniel realizes the situation is extremely dangerous. He jumps up and grabs the lantern, stepping in solvent in the process. (We all know solvent dissolves shoe soles.) As he nears the top rung of the steps, he slips.

The lantern smashes, Daniel gets splashed with kerosene. Flaming kerosene runs everywhere. Daniel is on fire. Liquid fire flows down into the galley. Within seconds, the boat is a blaze. Daniel fights desperately against the flames. Dreammaker's entire companionway is engulfed. Sounds of approaching SIRENS fill the air.

EXT. MAINE HARBOUR - NIGHT

Volunteer firemen in boats fight the fire. Large pumps pour thousands of gallons of water into Dreammaker's open hatches. The boat starts to list, then finally sink.

INT. HARBOURMASTER'S OFFICE - MORNING

It's more like a shack. The HARBOURMASTER, an older man, talks on the phone.

> HARBOURMASTER
> Boys were saying it had Canadian
> registration numbers on her hull.

He looks out into the harbour. All that's still visible of Dreammaker is her mast sticking a few feet above the water.

> HARBOURMASTER (CONT'D)
> No. They had to sink her to save
> the other boats that was moored up
> by her.

He looks down at a piece of paper on which some letters and numbers are written.

> HARBOURMASTER (CONT'D)
> Papa, Tango, Bravo, six, four, three,
> seven. That's right, Sheriff, Canadian.
> That's right.

He writes something down.

> HARBOURMASTER (CONT'D)
> Okay then. What's that? No. No sur-
> vivors. Fire might have started below,

maybe a heater or somethin' like that.
That's right. I don't suppose, if there's
anyone on board, they'd mind waiting
a day or two. Okay then. We'll see
you in a couple days. Bye.

He hangs up and pivots his chair to open the door to the shack.

> HARBOURMASTER (CONT'D)
> (yells out to someone in the harbour)
> It's going to be a couple days before
> they get down here! We gotta keep
> folks away from there!

EXT. MAINE MARINA – DAY

A volunteer out in the harbour fishes a cap out of the water. It's
Daniel's grandfather's.

> VOLUNTEER
> I found his hat! "James Tanner,
> Lunenburg, NS."

INT. NSP REPAIR YARD OFFICE – DAY

Josef is on the phone.

> JOSEF SORENSEN
> Ya morning, John. Say, I jus' spoke to
> da Harbourmaster here, he jus' got off
> da phone with a fella down in Maine.
> John, dere's been a fire.

EXT. NSP REPAIR YARD – DAY

John is down at the repair yard getting more details.

> JOHN GREEK
> You say they don't think he made
> it off?

> JOSEF SORENSEN
> No. Dere's no sign of him, so day
> say. The poor bastard! What's a fella
> to do?

Both men are visibly shaken.

> JOHN GREEK
> We go bring him home.

EXT. CHESTER YACHT CLUB - DAY

John's truck pulls into the parking lot. Richard sees John and waves.
Candace, Chad, and Dean are there as well.

> RICHARD
> Nice to see you, John. You up for a
> sail? We're just about to head out.

John's eyes are red from crying. He looks at Richard and the others.

> JOHN GREEK
> Thought you should know. Thar's
> been a terrible accident. Seems
> Daniel's boat caught fire last night.

Everyone freezes in shock.

                    RICHARD
        Oh my God. . .

                    JOHN GREEK
        They had to scuttle his boat to save
        the rest of the harbour. Thar's no sign
        of the boy. They're thinkin' he's still
        on board.

Dean holds onto Candace CANDACE
        They sunk it -- with Daniel still
        on board!?

The thought makes everyone pause as they take in the horrific
news. John's tears start to flow again.

                    JOHN GREEK
        I figure, the least I can do is go down
        an' help raise the boat. If he's there,
        I'll bring him home.

Richard takes Candace in his arms to comfort her.

                    RICHARD
        You won't be alone, I'm coming
        with you.

EXT. MAINE MARINA - DAY

A barge is out in the harbour. A diver breaks the surface and gives
a hand signal. The SHERIFF, Richard, John, and Candace stand by
watching. The two-way radio in the sheriff's car crackles to life.

SHERIFF

Excuse me.

CANDACE

Did they find Daniel?

RICHARD

No, not yet. Too dangerous, the divers
can't search inside the boat, too many
lines to get tangled in.

The sheriff returns, nervously scratching his head.

SHERIFF

I just got some interesting news.
Might be a good day after all.

RICHARD

What is it?

SHERIFF

That call on the radio. It seems there's
a young fella in the hospital down
the road who has no I.D, burns to his
back and arms, and speaks with some
kinda funny accent.

CANDACE

Daniel!?

SHERIFF

Caucasian male, early twenties,
blonde hair, about six foot.

CANDACE

That has to be him!

JOHN GREEK

Sounds like it! Little bugger must
have barely made it out.

SHERIFF

I'd be interested in talkin' to this
Daniel. Boys here figured the fire
might have been purposely set.

RICHARD

Why would he do that?

SHERIFF

Oh, I don't know, suicide, insurance,
you name it. I've seen people do some
pretty strange things.

INT. HOSPITAL WARD – DAY

The sheriff has finished questioning Daniel for now.

RICHARD

What did he say?

SHERIFF

He says it was an accident. His
word against whatever we find at
this point.

Dean Eilertson

RICHARD

Of course. Believe me this kid is
not suicidal.

SHERIFF

With him in here, we'll still want
to check out his story. He won't
be going any place for at least a
couple days.

RICHARD

Can we at least see him, talk to him?

The Sheriff gives a nod then leaves. Richard lets Candace go
into the room first. Daniel is resting. His eyes open as he senses
someone looking at him.

CANDACE

Hello, stranger.
What happened Daniel? We thought
you were dead.

Tears stream down Candaces face. At first Daniel can't find the
words to answer her.

DANIEL

. . . I was too miserable without you.

CANDACE

But why this? You've got so much to
live for.

>   DANIEL
>   Candace, it was an accident. I wasn't
>   trying to kill myself. I was trying to
>   fix my damn motor!

Daniel pulls a folded piece of charred paper from under his covers.
He gently places it in Candace's hand.

>   DANIEL (CONT'D)
>   My plan was to sail back, then give
>   you this in hopes that I could steal
>   you back from that new boyfriend
>   of yours.

>   CANDACE
>   David's not my boyfriend! He's my
>   cousin. Daniel, I only want to be with
>   you. I love you.

Daniel gets a strange look.

>   DANIEL
>   Your cousin?

>   CANDACE
>   Did you hear the rest of what I said?

Candace opens the piece of paper. It's the drawing she gave him.
Within its folds is a gold ring.

EXT. MAINE MARINA - DAY

Divers are out of the water. A compressor chugs away. Air bubbles
rise to the surface. Richard explains the procedure to the others.

RICHARD

They're pumping air down into blad-
ders the divers have strapped to your
boat. If they can displace enough of
the water to get her to the surface
they'll be able to pump out the hull.
If this works, it won't be long.

JOHN GREEK

They say she looks uglier than a bug's
rear! Still, sinking her put the fire out
fast enough that all she's maybe got is
surface damage. That could make her
very salvageable.

Daniel stands watching, his good arm is around Candace. The mast
starts to rise up out of the water. The burnt remains of Dreammaker
break to the surface. Everything is a blackened mess, including the
tattered, charred remains of the sails. Seaweed hangs clinging to
everything. But the boat appears intact!

SUPER: The Stewart family paid for the salvage work on Dreammaker
and had it brought back up to Lunenburg as a wedding gift.

SUPER: After the wedding, Candace and Daniel repaired and
repainted their boat throughout the following winter. With a new
set of sails, compliments of David, they relaunched Dreammaker
in the spring of 1951. The rest, as they say, is history.

SUPER: The fire was ruled an accident.

ROLL CREDITS

EXT. AMALFI COAST, NERANO, ITALY, 1951 – DAY

Waves wash up along the shoreline of the tiny Italian fishing village. It's a beautiful sunny day, the kind when everyone is glad to be alive.

Just offshore lies Daniel's majestic sailboat. It has the classic lines of an old east coast "salt banker" from the early 1930s. Only now her hull is a dark forest-green, with varnished wood trim. Its polished brass fittings sparkle in the bright afternoon sun.

The ship's anchor falls into the clear turquoise waters. Painted in gold just back of the anchor chain port is the boat's name: Dreammaker. The grinding of the anchor chain echoes back to shore as it pays out and then stops.

Two people on board hug in celebration.

                    CANDACE
          This is so gorgeous!

She laughs as she steps onto the stern and dives off into the turquoise water.

Candace surfaces. She is so happy.

                CANDACE (CONT'D)
          Daniel, come on!

Daniel pulls off his shirt, unties a halyard, and takes a running jump. He swings way out over the water. At the farthest point of the arc, he releases the line.

                    DANIEL
          Yahoo!

Daniel flies through the air. Candace laughs.

SPLASH!

Daniel surfaces. The two embrace and kiss.

> CANDACE
> Congratulations, Captain Tanner.
> You must be very proud.

> DANIEL
> Welcome to Italy, Mrs. Tanner.

EXT. CAFÉ TERRASE

A table of old Italian men stop playing their game of poker to take in the antics.

EXT. MILITARY CEMETERY — DAY

Daniel places his dad's service medals on a simple wooden cross marked "Corporal Tanner." Rows of similar crosses mark the graves of many more. He rejoins a man he and Candace met a few days earlier. Locals told them he was part of the local resistance during the war. Who, as it turns out, not only knew Daniel's father but had fought along beside him as well.

EXT. DREAMMAKER — DAY

Candace closes Daniel's ledger, stands up, and looks out towards shore. Daniel who is being brought back out to their boat in a little rowboat being rowed by the man who just took Daniel to see the cemetery. She waves.

Smiling. He waves back.

FADE OUT

CPSIA information can be obtained
at www.ICGtesting.com
Printed in the USA
LVHW111254050119
602875LV00001B/3/P